Luisa

THE FINAL NOVELLA in
a JEWISH FAMILY SAGA series

USA Today Bestselling Author
ROBERTA KAGAN

CHAPTER 1

1906 Germany

Luisa Eisenreich's face was red with anger as she packed all her things. Her hands were trembling, and she had tears in her eyes. But she couldn't stop to cry. She had to get out of there. How could she go on living with her mother in the maid's quarters of the Horwitzes' home after what Noam Horwitz, their son, had done to her?

Noam was his parents' pride and joy, their precious son. But in secret, he'd been her lover. He was handsome and rich. He was cultured; he'd been to the theater and the opera. He even played piano. His manners and his way of speaking left her breathless with longing.

She was only fifteen when they met. A shy, quiet girl who no one would have called pretty. Her father had abandoned her and her mother, leaving them destitute. Her mother had no choice but to take the position of housekeeper working for the Horwitzes who allowed her to bring her daughter, Luisa, with her to live at the their home. She'd even helped Mrs. Eisenreich to register Luisa at the local school. There were students who were less affluent than the others in her class at school, but no one was as poor as Luisa. And she always felt so alone.

That was until the day she met Noam. He had come home from college to visit his parents. And he was the first boy who'd ever paid her any attention. She drank that attention in like a woman parched in the desert. She needed him so badly that she ignored the fact a real relationship between them would be impossible. And because she wanted to believe him so badly when he said that he cared for her, she was completely sold. He'd promised her that it didn't matter to him that she was only the maid's daughter. He told her she was beautiful and that she was everything he was looking for in a wife. And she'd willingly gone to his bed.

Every day was like heaven for her. She imagined herself marrying Noam and becoming one of the Horwitzes. The girls in town wouldn't snub her anymore. They would want to be her friend because she was a part of an influential family and they adored her. But then Noam had returned from college with a girl, Ann. Ann was a pretty Jewish girl from a good family who Noam planned to marry. Luisa finally found a way to be alone with Noam. She asked him what he was doing, and how he could have done this to her. He just smiled and shook his head. "I thought you knew we were just play acting."

"Play acting? You said you were in love with me."

"I thought that was what you wanted to hear," he said. "You know how it is. Girls need to hear 'I love you' in order to feel right about sleeping with a boy."

His answers left Luisa shaken up. *He has changed. That witch, that Jewish witch, has cast a spell on him. My Noam is not the same man. Something has happened and he has changed completely. He wasn't like the other Jews before, but he is certainly acting like one of them now. I know it's that woman, that Jewish witch.* He seemed to forget holding her in his arms, taking her innocence, and promising to love her forever. Luisa wished she could go back in time to when she and Noam were lovers. When she could feel the truth of his affection in his every touch. Back to the time before he was bewitched by that other woman, that Jewish woman, who stole his heart from her.

She looked around the room. There wasn't much to pack. A few worn dresses her mother had made for her. A faux pearl hair ornament she'd stolen from the handbag of one the girls in her class. And . . . the dresses that hung in the closet. They haunted her. They were by far the most beautiful things she'd ever owned. Luisa rubbed her eyes hard, pushing away the tears. And flung open the closet door. As she looked at the dresses, she remembered how grateful she'd felt the day Frau Birnbaum had given them to her.

Frau Birnbaum was a friend of Frau Horwitz. She was a wealthy woman whose husband owned a women's clothing factory. The dresses had belonged to her daughter, Goldie, who was a fellow student at the same school that Luisa attended. Goldie was beautiful and popular and everything Luisa wished she could be. But she was also cruel and selfish. She made no secret of the fact that she looked down on Luisa. Taking the dresses that Frau Birnbaum had given her from her closet, she lay them on the bed. *To think, I once thought Goldie Birnbaum's old clothes were beautiful.*

Tears fell like a river down Luisa's cheeks. There was no suppressing them anymore. The dresses were like new. And . . . they were quite beautiful, but she thought, *Now, the idea of wearing Goldie's used clothes makes me sick. It was Frau Birnbaum; she was the problem. She was always trying to do something nice for someone. Not like her daughter, Goldie. Goldie is a monster. But in her efforts, she always made things worse. It would have been better if Frau Birnbaum had just left me alone. Before the incident with Goldie and the dresses, no one talked to me at school, but no one laughed at me either. It took me weeks to feel comfortable wearing one of those dresses. I felt like they were too fine for someone like me. Then once Noam fell in love with me, everything changed. I convinced myself it was all right for me to wear a fancy*

3

dress, because a boy like Noam would never fall in love with a girl who wasn't worthy. I put one of the dresses on, then I looked in the mirror, and instead of seeing myself, a skinny girl with a bad complexion, I saw a girl like Goldie, pretty and popular, smiling back at me. I was so proud of how I looked that day when I went to school. And everything was fine until Goldie saw me. She recognized the dress immediately. Probably because she'd had it made for her. I didn't want to confront her, but there was no other way out of the cafeteria. She called out to me when she saw me—"Luisa." Then she humiliated me by telling everyone that I was wearing her old clothes. She and her friends laughed at me as she told them I really didn't belong at this school. The only reason I was permitted to attend was because I was the daughter of a maid who lived in her mother's friend's home which was located within the district. Goldie called me a gutter rat and said I deserved to be in a filthy poor section of town. I couldn't look at their faces. But I heard their laughter, and it made me feel like dirt.

She touched the soft material of a cashmere dress. *I hate Frau Birnbaum for giving me these dresses. I despise Goldie Birnbaum, and Mrs. Horwitz too. I'm sure she demanded her son marry another Jew. I hate Ann for being what I am not. And I hate my mother for moving us into this rich woman's house and sending me to school in this wealthy neighborhood. I don't fit in here. I'll never fit in here. But . . . Noam . . . I want to, but I can't hate Noam.*

Her face still stung from the slap her mother had given when she ran into her room in shock after she saw Noam Horwitz had come home from college with Ann, his fiancée.

"I told you he would never marry you," Luisa's mother had said. "I told you he would sleep with you and then marry one of his own. Another Jew like him. They stick together."

"I hate you, Mother," was all she could say. But then she'd lain in her bed and wept because her mother's words had rung true.

A bitter taste came into her mouth as she thought of her mother on her hands and knees scrubbing the Horwitzes' floors. *I will never come back here. I would rather die,* she thought as

4

she took all her mother's savings and stuffed the money into her pocketbook. Then she closed her suitcase and quickly left.

She'd left in a huff, but now that she was alone at the bus stop, she was frightened and a little lost. At fifteen, she'd never been on her own. *I'll have to find a job, and a place to live. But I need to gather as much money as I can get my hands on.*

Before she caught a bus out of the area, she walked to a secondhand clothing store that she saw at the end of the street. She waited until there were no customers in the shop, then she took the dresses Frau Birnbaum had given her out of her suitcase, and laid them on the counter. The shop owner's eyes flew open. She had to admit the dresses were of good quality and in impeccable condition.

"Still," she said, "I must resell them, and in order to make money I cannot pay you what they are worth. I'll pay you what I can."

Luisa nodded.

The shop owner handed her a nice sum of money. "This is the best I can do for all of them."

Luisa counted the money. Nodding in acceptance, she stuffed the money into her handbag right beside the money she'd taken from her mother and left the store. Luisa knew where to go. She'd grown up in a poor section of Berlin, and she knew that rent would be cheap there. So she boarded a bus and was on her way.

Luisa rented a room in a boarding house for women. It was far from luxurious. Just a bed, a dresser, and a desk with a lamp. The furniture was worn. But at least she had her own place and wouldn't have to face anyone in the Horwitz family again, unless she wanted to.

After putting her suitcase on the floor, she went downstairs and out into the street to visit a small grocer where she purchased some food. Then she went back into her room, and except for using the bathroom down the hall, she didn't leave her room for two days. During that time, she lay on her cot, which was hard and uncomfortable compared to the bed she'd slept in at the Horwitzes' home. It took some getting used to, but she knew she could not go back. She thought about her mother who she knew would be very upset when she found Luisa gone. *Serves her right for slapping me.*

Then she thought about Noam. At first, she was furious with him. *How could he have lain with me and then proposed to another girl?* Luisa punched the pillow on her bed and kicked her feet. But after her anger left her, she found that she was sad, very sad. It felt as if all her dreams evaporated in a matter of hours. She'd truly allowed herself to believe she was going to be the next Frau Horwitz. That she was going to live with Noam in his room and be accepted by his family. *I am a fool,* she thought bitterly. *He made a fool of me, just like Goldie Birnbaum and her mother did. Jews. This is the way Jews treat other people.*

CHAPTER 2

1913

Over the year since Luisa left, she had several jobs which she was unable to keep. She drifted from factory work to waiting tables. She had no marketable skills and had not even finished high school. She'd recently been fired for stealing again. *Well, how can they expect me not to steal? I don't make enough money to live.*

Finally, she wrote to her mother and apologized for taking all the money she'd saved. But in her letter, she told her mother she would never return to the Horwitzes' home. How could she? She could never face Noam and his wife. And if she went back to that neighborhood, she would have to endure Goldie taunting her again. No, she would continue to live on her own in this small room in the woman's hotel.

Then she got another job working in a factory. It was hard work, and to make matters worse she didn't earn enough money to pay her bills. One night as she stood at her machine, she overheard two girls talking.

"It's easier to find work in Vienna," one of them said.

"Oh? What kind of work?"

"All kinds, I hear."

"My boyfriend and I are going there. Come with us," the girl suggested. "He has an automobile; we'll be driving there on Sunday. All it would cost you is money for gas."

"I couldn't. My mutti is sick. I have to stay here in Germany and take care of her."

Luisa had nothing to lose. She decided that her luck was not good in Germany. "I'll go," she said. "I'll pay for the gas."

Both girls looked up. They stared at Luisa as if they'd never noticed her before.

"I suppose it would be all right," the one said. "You say you would pay for the gas?"

"Yes, I will."

"All right, then. We're going on Sunday."

They made arrangements to meet in front of the woman's boarding house where Luisa lived.

And so, on Sunday morning, she checked out of her room and left for Vienna.

Vienna was a beautiful city, and being in a new place gave her a burst of hope. She was encouraged. With the help of a waitress at a diner she found another hotel for women where she rented a cheap room. But she still needed work. She found jobs in restaurants and factories. It wasn't much different than Berlin. She even found a job in a chocolate shop, but she ate too much of the chocolate and was fired.

Seven years passed during which Luisa struggled. She was always looking for work, either because she'd been fired or because she needed better pay to make her bills. One Sunday morning she got up and looked through the want ads in the local paper like she always did, when her eyes fell upon an ad that caught her interest.

Job Available: We are looking for a woman to work as housekeeper for a Jewish men's university dormitory. Followed by an address and contact information.

She tore the address out of the paper and stuffed it into her handbag. Luisa thought of Noam. He'd lived in a Jewish dorm when he was in school. And she wanted to see what it might feel like to be in a Jewish dormitory. The idea of experiencing what his life had been like when he was away at college intrigued her. Sometimes she hated him. He'd hurt her deeply. But he'd also been her first man, and somewhere deep within her she still loved him too. *While working at this job I could listen to the young men as they talk. What if I could learn from them? What if I could find out how I failed him? Maybe I could change? Then I could write to him, and perhaps by now he's grown tired of Ann.* She let out a sigh. *Imagine me going back to the Horwitzes' home with Noam on my arm. I can hear him telling his mother that he had made a mistake marrying Ann and that he planned to divorce her and marry me. I can just see my mother's face when I tell her that she is no longer to be the cleaning woman. She is the mother of the future Mrs. Horwitz.*

At twenty-two, Luisa had grown into a woman. She dressed carefully in a dark skirt and white blouse for her interview. She wanted to look her best. In some strange way, in the back of her mind, she thought Noam might be there. Of course, in reality, she knew he wouldn't. He had gone to school in England and had graduated by now. The awful truth was he was probably married to Ann, and the two of them were probably living at his parents' home. *They are probably sleeping together in the bed where he made love to me.* She grunted. *Well, it doesn't do me any good to think about him. He won't be at this job interview. But I do need work, and I will have a chance to see what a Jewish dormitory is like. It will be interesting to see what his day-to-day life might have been like when he was away at school.* Even though it had been seven years since he'd held her in his arms, she thought of him every day.

Once she was dressed, Luisa looked into the mirror, and she combed her hair carefully into a knot at the back of her neck. Then she put on just a hint of lipstick. Lipstick was hard to come by. Luisa didn't have money to waste on frivolities like cosmetics. This tube of half-used lipstick had lasted her seven years. She'd stolen it from a store when she was living in

ROBERTA KAGAN

Berlin. There was plenty left because she only used it for the most important of occasions.

When she arrived at the interview at the dormitory, a group of women were seated in a large room waiting to be called in. Luisa sat down beside a young girl with dark brown hair. As the sun shot rays through the large picture window, the girl's hair lit up with auburn highlights.

"'Allo," the girl with the auburn hair said.

"'Allo," Luisa answered.

"I'm Paula, Paula Wolff."

"Luisa Eisenreich."

"Nice to meet you."

"Likewise."

Luisa began to fill out the papers she had been given.

They did not speak for a moment, then Paula said, "It's strange to be applying for a job as a housekeeper for a Jewish boy's dormitory. Would you believe me if I told you that I have never met a Jew? I mean I've seen them on the street and all. The scary old men with their long beards and strange side-burns. And their black hats."

"Yes, I've seen them too," Luisa said. "They are scary."

"But have you ever talked to one?"

"Actually, I have. Not the ones with the long beards. Not those. There are different kinds. The ones I knew were really rich and dressed very stylishly. My mother was a maid for that Jewish family. I hated them."

"Why? Were you frightened of them?"

"No. It wasn't that."

"Then why did you hate them?"

"I can't tell you." Luisa turned away.

"I'm sorry. I didn't mean to pry. Sometimes I get carried away."

"It's all right. Really," Luisa said.

Paula was called in to be interviewed first. Her interview took about fifteen minutes. Then it was Luisa's turn.

She walked into a pleasant well-lit office, where she found a slender, middle-aged man wearing a nice suit seated behind a desk. He took the application from Luisa and read it.

"Frau Eisenreich," he said, "you have had several jobs in the last six months. May I ask why?"

She shrugged. "I don't know. It wasn't my fault. I haven't done anything wrong . . ."

"I see. But according to this paperwork, you were let go from each of these positions."

"I was replaced by family or friends of the boss that needed a job."

"Every time? There are four jobs here. Each time this same thing happened to you?" He frowned. "It's rather odd. Don't you think?"

She shrugged. When she'd first come into the room, she thought the man was handsome, but now as he was speaking, she was finding him repulsive.

"All right," he said. Then added, "I'll keep your paperwork on file. And I'll be in touch if anything opens."

"But isn't there a job open right now?"

"No, there was an opening when I placed the ad in the paper, but I am sorry to say that I already filled it."

"But then why are you interviewing?"

"I didn't want to send you home without meeting you. I thought it would be rude. But, I hired the girl who interviewed right before you."

Luisa's mouth fell open in shock. She was disappointed. He'd hired the girl she met who had called herself Paula. *She is least five years younger than me. And probably had less job experience. But she also hasn't been fired from so many jobs either.*

"I'm sorry, Frau Eisenreich. But as I said, I'll keep your application on file. You never know, she may not work out."

"Hmmm," Luisa grunted. *I know a lie when I hear one,* she thought. *He just wants me to get out of here, so he is giving me hope.* Inside she was raging. There were so many things she wanted to say. Luisa stood up and looked around the room, her eyes coming to rest on the mahogany desk. And the man who sat behind it in his expensive wool suit. She eyed the handmade Persian rug, and the thick black leather chairs. *Rich Jews. Rich Jews always treat me badly. They think they're better than Germans. I'd like to teach them a lesson or two.*

"I am glad you didn't hire me. I wouldn't want to work for Jews anyway." She spat at him, and then she turned and left.

Her hands were shaking as she walked outside the building and turned to walk toward home. She would have liked to take the bus, but she didn't have the extra money to waste on carfare. So she'd have to walk two miles.

"Luisa!" a voice called out. Luisa turned to see Paula walking toward her. Luisa turned and began walking away. She tried to walk as fast as she could. Luisa didn't want to speak to Paula. She didn't want to hear the other girl gloat over how she beat Luisa out and got the job. "Wait up, Luisa," Paula said, running and then catching up with Luisa and walking beside her.

"What do you want?" Luisa asked curtly.

"I want to take you out for lunch. My treat. Will you please allow me to?" Paula said. She was out of breath from running.

I don't have any food back at my room, and I am very hungry. I still have a little money, but I should save as much as I can until I can find work. So if this girl is willing to buy me a meal, why not take her up on it? She glanced at Paula, who was smiling, not in a gloating way, but in a friendly way. "All right," Luisa conceded. "I'd like that."

They walked side by side until they came to a small, inexpensive-looking restaurant. "Would this place be all right?" Paula asked. "I am afraid I can't afford anything expensive."

"Yes, it would be fine."

They went inside and sat down. The owner came to the table to take their orders. He was an older man with a friendly smile and a heavy, dark mustache. Paula ordered two bowls of soup and a hunk of hearty peasant bread. She gave the owner a bright smile which he returned.

"I know you got the job," Luisa said. "That idiot Jew in the interview told me."

Paula nodded. "Yes," was all she said.

"Congratulations. So, now you get to clean up after a bunch of spoiled Jewish boys."

"I needed the work," Paula offered. "I would have taken anything."

"Do you live with your family?" Luisa asked.

"No, I'm on my own. My parents died when I was young. My father died when I was only six, my mother when I was eleven."

"Are you an only child too? I am an only child," Luisa said.

"No. I had four brothers and sisters, but they all died except for my older brother. He's a handsome artist. And you know what? The last time we spoke, he told me that he is planning to attend the Academy of Fine Arts in Vienna. But he doesn't have any money to help me out, so I must manage on my own. Once he becomes famous, I am sure he will be very generous with me."

"Do you see him often?"

"No, I never see him. He is like that. He will be completely unreachable for years and then suddenly he will surface again. I suppose all fine artists are a bit quirky," Paula said, smiling sadly. "I wish he would contact me. He knows I am here in Vienna, but he doesn't write or come by."

"What's his name?" Luisa asked, fascinated with the story of the young, handsome artist.

"I call him Adalwolf. Someday, perhaps you'll meet him."

"I have often wished I had brothers or sisters," Luisa mused.

The soup arrived. It was hot and delicious. And somehow,

even though Paula had been chosen for the job over Luisa, Luisa found that she liked Paula.

"I'm new here in Vienna. And I could use a friend," Luisa admitted.

It was a little after twelve noon, and the restaurant began to get busy with local people in need of an inexpensive meal. The owner was the only employee. He sat the diners, prepared the food, and served. He seemed to be overwhelmed.

After Luisa and Paula finished eating, in her quiet and unassuming way, Paula asked the owner if he could use some help at the restaurant.

"I could, but I couldn't afford to pay much," he said. "I have to keep my prices down, or I won't have any business."

"I completely understand." Paula said then she turned to Luisa. "What do you think? Would you like to work here?"

"I would."

The owner looked at Luisa. Then he looked at Paula. It was clear he would rather have hired Paula, but he agreed to take Luisa on as his hostess and waitress.

The two girls left the restaurant. As they walked toward the bus, Luisa said, "Thank you for lunch. And I want you to know that I appreciate your getting me a job. That was awfully nice of you," Luisa said sincerely.

"I am so glad I was able to help." Paula said, then she added, "We should try to meet once a week. Either at your flat or at mine. I could use a friend too."

"I would like that," Luisa said as Paula boarded a bus.

Luisa stood for a moment and watched the bus pull away, and then she walked home.

CHAPTER 3

At first Luisa did well at her job. She arrived on time and worked hard. The restaurant was busy during the afternoon, and although the prices were inexpensive, she began to feel that the owner should be paying her better. As the months went by, she began to resent him. The resentment grew. She was sure he was getting rich on her hard work. And once again, as she'd done before, she began stealing. If the owner knew, he never mentioned it.

One day each week, Luisa and Paula would have dinner together and play cards. Luisa looked forward to it. And finally, one night when the two girls had been drinking heavily, Luisa told Paula about Noam.

"You slept with a Jew? I can't believe it," Paula said. "What did his, you know, look like? I mean, they cut half of it off when the boys are babies? Don't they? I mean, I've heard that."

"Yes, they do. And his, you know, looked a lot different than regular fellows."

They both giggled. "Did you really love him?" Paula asked.

"Yes. I did. And he broke my heart. I never told anyone before. I mean not how much he really hurt me. I think my mother knew, but she was so cold and not very understanding."

"I don't know what you could have seen in him. The Jew boys at the dormitory are spoiled. They're slobs, and they act like children," Paula said. "They make messes everywhere that they don't clean up."

"I'm not surprised. I can imagine that they do. My mother was the maid at Noam's house; that's how I met him."

"Oh, my friend," Paula said, patting her on the back. "They are a selfish bunch."

"Jews or men?" Luisa asked.

"Both." The girls laughed together.

Then Paula asked, "Why did you want this job at the dormitory? Wouldn't it have reminded you of Noam?"

"Yes, but I wanted to know more about his life. I wanted to see where he lived, and how he lived when he was away at school. It was just a curiosity, I guess. I was his lover, but I knew nothing about his life. Not really."

"Well, I can take you to the dorm during the day when the boys are in classes so you can see it. Would you like that?"

"I would. But it would have to be on a day that I was off from work."

"When is your next day off?"

"Tuesday."

"That's perfect for me. I'm working but they trust me, and they allow me to work at my own pace. It's like not having a boss. But don't go through the main building. Come through the dorm. It's best that the administration doesn't find out about this."

"Of course," Luisa said. "So where should I meet you?"

They arranged a time and a meeting place.

"I'll even help you clean," Luisa said.

"You are such a good friend. And by the way, I am given free lunch in the cafeteria on the days that I work. I'll go and get my food and ask for a little extra. Then we can share."

Luisa squeezed Paula's hand. "I'll be there," she said.

CHAPTER 4

Paula was waiting for Luisa when she arrived. "This is it," she said. "As always, the boys left the bathroom a mess."

"I'll help you. First, can I see one of the bedrooms."

"Of course, but they aren't all empty. Some of the boys take later classes. So, I have to find one where the boys have already gone."

They knocked on a door. "Maid service," Paula called out.

"Can you come back later?" a sleepy voice came from behind the door.

"Yes. Thank you," Paula said, then she gave Luisa a look. They went to another door. She knocked. "Maid service," Paula said.

There was no answer. Luisa reached for the door. Paula stopped her hand. "Maid service," she said again. There was no answer. Paula nodded and Luisa opened the door. They walked into the room. There were two unmade beds inside. Beside each of the beds was a desk. Heaps of books and clothes were strewn about the floor. Crunched-up papers lay all around the waste basket. An empty plate with cheese residue stuck to it sat on one of the desks, and cracker crumbs were scattered on the floor.

"Slobs," Paula said.

"Yes, they certainly are," Luisa answered, "but most men are. Aren't they?"

"Not all the boys are this way. I have to admit some of them are nice. Some even try to keep their rooms up. Others sometimes get me food when they go shopping. And then there are the ones that are just selfish and sloppy."

Luisa touched the sheet and the pillowcase on one of the beds. She closed her eyes. She imagined that Noam had slept there. And without warning she began to cry. Paula looked at her. "I am thinking this was a mistake," Paula said.

"Yes, perhaps. I mean it hurts to imagine Noam at all," Luisa said wistfully. "But at least I've seen the room. Now I will no longer wonder what it was like for him at college."

"Let's go," Paula suggested, threading her arm through Luisa's.

Luisa nodded. As they walked down the hall, they heard female laughter coming from one of the rooms. Luisa wiped her tears away with the back of her hand. "There's a girl in one of the rooms."

"Yes, it's against the rules, but it happens all the time. The boys bring them in, and as long as no one says anything they get away with it."

Luisa didn't want to tell Paula that she was sorry she'd gone to the dormitory. *It was a mistake,* Luisa decided. She would not return there ever. And she was glad she had not gotten the job. It would have been far too painful for her to work there each day.

Each week Luisa continued to spend an evening with Paula, and as time passed, their friendship grew stronger.

CHAPTER 5

1914

On the first of August, a blisteringly hot day, Germany entered the Great War. All of the patrons at the restaurant where Luisa worked were talking about it. They were excited and certain that Austria and Germany, her ally, would be victorious. But Luisa was not so sure. She was worried. The very idea of being at war frightened her. So, that evening, after the restaurant closed, Luisa went to Paula's flat. She needed to talk to someone about her fears.

"What a pleasant surprise," Paula said when she opened the door to find Luisa there. "Come in." She smiled. "Did I get the days wrong? I didn't think we were scheduled to meet until next Wednesday."

"No, you were right. I came to talk to you because I am worried about the war. I'm sure you've heard about it."

"Of course, I've heard. But I'm not worried. Everyone knows that the Russians are not as smart as we are. They're nothing but big brutes. The Serbians are the same. And the French and British don't scare me either. None of them have the intelligence of the Austrians and the Germans. You needn't worry." Paula smiled warmly. "Here, come sit down and have a glass of schnapps." She took a bottle out of the pantry and filled two glasses. "This bottle was given to me by one of the boys who stays in the dormitory. He gave it me because I never told on him when he brought his girlfriend to his room." She laughed a little. "Good thing he was a bad boy, huh?"

Luisa nodded. "Good thing. Because this bottle is certainly coming in rather handy right now."

They had a few glasses of the schnapps. They talked. Paula soothed her fears, and by the end of the evening, Luisa felt better.

CHAPTER 6

1916 Winter

The British Navy set up a blockade preventing food delivery to Germany and Austria. This made it difficult for Luisa's boss to purchase enough food to keep the restaurant open. He didn't want to close the business. So instead of closing outright, he went day by day. When he was able to purchase food, he opened. But when he was unable to acquire enough supplies, he closed for the day. Money was tight for Luisa. Because the restaurant was closed so often, her income decreased, but her bills did not. She still had to pay rent every month. And the same was true for the restaurant owner. Luisa knew he didn't need her. He could do all the work alone. He'd done it before he hired her. She was afraid he would let her go. Finally, after several sleepless nights, she went to talk to him about her fears. He told her that he knew she needed the job. And he didn't want to fire her. So the best he could do was to cut her pay until things improved.

Luisa had been barely getting by before, and now she was in real financial trouble. She had no skills to speak of, but as the men left the city to go to war, the jobs that they'd held in the factories opened. Luisa found work, and for a while she held the two positions. She worked at the restaurant during the day when it was open. At night she worked on an assembly line. But even with the extra money she was earning, it was impossible to purchase enough food. Most nights she prepared turnip stew for herself.

The factories were now filled with women working the jobs that men had once held. These women had once been either single, or housewives and mothers. They had a lot in common and enjoyed a certain camaraderie. Luisa had never been a popular girl. And even now, at this new job, she knew she didn't fit in. She lived alone and had no boyfriend. In her mind this justified the fact that she was lazy when it came to personal hygiene. She didn't bathe often and didn't brush her teeth daily. When she walked into a room at the factory, the other women giggled and whispered among themselves. Luisa's feelings were hurt. She wanted to be liked but wasn't willing to ask the others what they were laughing at. Each day when Luisa went into the lunchroom, no one would sit next to her. If she sat down beside one of the girls, that girl got up and moved.

Then one afternoon a new girl was hired to work at the factory. She was not like the others. The other girls giggled and covered their mouths with their hands to hide their laughter when Luisa walked into the lunchroom, but this one didn't laugh. She turned to Luisa and said, "Luisa, you smell. Everyone is laughing at you because you smell. Go home today after work and take a bath. Wash your hair, for good-ness' sake. It's stuck to your head with oil. Didn't your mother teach you to keep yourself clean?"

The other women laughed openly now. They nudged each other and laughed even harder. The new girl had spoken the words they could not.

Luisa was appalled. Suddenly her mind flashed back to Goldie Birnbaum, the Jewish girl she'd known in school, who had embarrassed and humiliated her. "You're a dirty Jew," she said to the new girl.

"What?" the girl answered.

"You're a Jew."

"I am not," the girl answered. "I don't know what you're talking about. You don't make any sense. All I know is that you are filthy. You need to clean yourself up and take care to keep yourself clean. A girl, in the very nature of being a girl, must be clean. If you understand what I am trying to say," then she whispered, "Everyone can smell you when you have your monthly friend."

Someone let out a loud burst of laughter. And then Luisa was on her feet. She ran over to the new girl and knocked her onto the floor. Luisa began kicking the girl in the stomach. Someone screamed, and the foreman came into the lunch-room. He pulled Luisa off the new girl who was lying on the floor bleeding from her mouth.

"What is the meaning of this, Frau Eisenreich?" the foreman asked.

"She was making fun of me," Luisa said, "and she hit me first."

The foreman turned to the other girls. "What happened here?"

Several of the girls gave testimony against Luisa.

"It was all Luisa's fault. The new girl didn't do anything."

"Luisa started it. She hit the new girl first."

This made Luisa feel even worse. They all hated her. She could hear it in the way talked about her.

The foreman listened. Then he turned to Luisa. "We don't tolerate fighting here. You're fired."

CHAPTER 7

1917

Over the four years that Luisa had been in Austria, her friendship with Paula grew stronger. Their weekly meetings continued. She'd even felt close enough to Paula to ask her about her hygiene. And instead of laughing at Luisa, Paula was honest but kind.

"You are my best friend," Paula said, "and you know that I value our friendship very much. However, for your own sake, I think it would benefit you to bathe more often. To wash your hair as well."

"So, it's true? I smell bad?"

"Sometimes. But it's nothing a good bath and some pretty scented soap won't fix," Paula said. She winked. Then she went into the top drawer of her dresser and took out a bar of soap that was wrapped in beautiful pink paper. "I was saving this for a special occasion," she said, "but I want to give it to you."

Luisa felt the tears form in her eyes. "This is very kind of you. But I couldn't take it," she said.

"Of course you can. And I insist that you do. Now please take it," Paula said, handing the soap to Luisa.

"Thank you," Luisa said, taking the soap.

"Smell it. It smells like roses."

"Where did you get it?"

"It was a gift from my brother, Adalwolf. He gave it to me when I turned ten."

"You've saved it that long?" Luisa said. Then she added, "I couldn't take it."

"Don't start that again. I want you to have it. Please, take it."

Luisa smiled. Then she hugged Paula. "You are the sister I never had," she said. Luisa was the happiest she'd ever been in her life, during those years.

Even though the owner of the restaurant never offered to increase her pay back to the original amount, the few marks that she was able to steal from the restaurant till supplemented her income enough for her to get by. But then one morning she arrived at the restaurant to find that the owner was not there. In his place was a man of about forty who looked strong and capable.

"Who are you? And where is Herr Weber?" Luisa asked.

"I am Hans Weber, your old boss's son. My father is getting older. It's becoming too hard for him to work such long hours. I am taking over the restaurant, so I will be your new boss."

Luisa was uncomfortable with the change at work. She'd been working with Hans's father for several years now, and over that time they'd developed a rhythm. Often there was no need for words. They understood each other. When she placed an order, he knew what she meant without her explaining. Hans had never worked in a restaurant before, and now he had taken over his father's position in the kitchen and was cooking. He expected the order tickets that Luisa gave him to be precise, and he often yelled at her when there was a house full of customers. "Luisa, I'm not a mind reader. This ticket makes no sense," he would say. Hot blood rushed to her face. She was embarrassed. She wanted to run out of the restaurant so she didn't have to face the customers. But she needed the job.

Hans never took the blame for anything. If he made a mistake or burned an order, which he often did, he accused Luisa of the mishap. "You were bothering me. I had to listen to you, and now look what's happened. The entire order is ruined," he would say.

Most of the time the problems at the restaurant were not her fault, but it began to seem like every day she was being reprimanded. As the weeks passed, Luisa grew more and more disenchanted with her job. In fact, she was growing to hate it. She hated Hans, and the more he yelled at her, the more money she stole.

Then one morning about two months after Hans had taken over, Luisa arrived at work to find that Frau Weber, Han's wife, was now working at the restaurant.

"I've gone over our financials. And from what I surmise, the money box has been short every week since I arrived." Hans glared at Luisa. "And—" he hesitated, staring into her eyes for dramatic effect—"since I am not dipping *my* fingers in the till, I know you must be. So, I am letting you go. My wife is here now. She can do your job."

"Like hell she can," Luisa scoffed. Even though it was true that she had been stealing, she was angry. "The two of you have no idea as to how a restaurant is run. You mark my words, without me to help you, you'll lose this business in a few months."

"Get out," Hans said. "You don't keep yourself clean, and you're a thief to boot. Go home."

Luisa glared at him, and then at his wife. She shook her head, then she turned and left. This was the longest she'd ever worked at any job, and she felt lost without it. She went back to her room and tried to read, but she couldn't concentrate. Her feelings were deeply hurt. *If only I could speak to Hans's father. I would tell him that his son was ruining his business. But I don't know where they live or how to get in touch with him.* She had no appetite. In fact, she didn't eat all day. Instead, she sat staring out the window. That evening, as soon as she knew Paula would be home from work, she went to see her friend.

"I lost my job today," Luisa said.

"What happened?" Paula asked.

Luisa explained everything that had happened.

"You never told me anything about your old boss leaving."

"I know. I was hoping that he would change his mind and come back to work. His son is a real louse."

"Well, there are other jobs." Paula patted Luisa's hand. "Why don't you stay for dinner? I made some spatzel."

"Do you have enough for two?"

"We'll make do," Paula said.

CHAPTER 8

1918

After the daily exhaustive job searches that always ended in disappointment, Luisa ran out of money. She could not pay her rent. For a few weeks she moved in with Paula, but Paula's flat was small and cramped and not big enough for two. One morning she bought the Berlin paper and found several job openings. Living with Paula was putting a lot of strain on their friendship, so Luisa decided she would return to Germany. That night when Paula returned from work, she talked it over with her. "There were several job openings in the Berlin paper. I need work. I can't put you out like this anymore," Luisa said.

"I will miss you, but I agree, this place is too small for two people," Paula said. Then she added, "We'll keep in touch through letters, yes?"

"Of course, I'll write to you all the time." Luisa was feeling a heavy sense of loss. She was hoping that Paula would tell her that she didn't mind the cramped quarters. She was hoping Paula would beg her not to go.

"I know we will live near each other again someday,"

Paula assured her. "Perhaps I'll come to Germany or you'll return to Vienna."

"I hope so. I've enjoyed our friendship so much," Luisa said, fighting the tears. "You're the first real friend I've ever had. And I wish I could stay here in Vienna." She made one last attempt, hoping Paula would say, it's all right, you can stay. She waited for a few moments. Then she stood up and began to pack. Luisa turned to Paula and added, "I really do wish I could stay. But, without work I can't. I know there is no guarantee that I will find work in Berlin. But I know I can't find it here. At least not right now."

Paula said nothing. She just nodded.

CHAPTER 9

Before Luisa left, Paula loaned her money to rent a room when she got back to Berlin.

"Are you sure?" Luisa asked.

"You have no money, right?"

"Yes, right."

"Well, you have to have train fare and then to rent a room when you get there. So, here, take this," Paula said, handing her some money.

Luisa felt funny. Paula seemed to be losing patience with her. It seemed that she was glad to be rid of Luisa.

Luisa took the money and hugged her friend, then she took her suitcase and walked to the train. Once she was on board and alone, the tears began to flow down her face.

Luisa returned to Berlin and moved back to the boarding house where she'd lived before. She'd always been a good tenant, quiet, stayed out of trouble, and paid her rent on time. The woman who ran the boarding house remembered her, and she helped her to find a job. It was a miserable job, a filthy job cleaning blood, vomit, and feces, but it paid. So Luisa took it. She would be working as housekeeper at the hospital. And now with all the soldiers who were returning from the war, scared and broken, her job was secure.

Luisa was envious of the nurses, the way the soldiers leaned on them and shared secrets with them and fell in love with them. Not only that, but once again, she was an outcast. There was a camaraderie between the nurses that did not include her. Since she'd always felt like an outsider with everyone except Paula, she expected it. Still, she envied the easy way the nurses talked and laughed among themselves. *Someday, I will be a nurse. Someday, I'll be one of them, and then they'll accept me. I won't be the slob they call to clean up the messes. I am invisible to them. They don't even see me as a human being. That is unless they think I have done a poor job at cleaning a room or I am working too slow. Then they reprimand me and make me feel even more worthless.*

Luisa was very lonely. She let her personal hygiene slip again. It took effort to shower daily. It took effort to wash her hair. When she was not at work, she lay on her cot and slept. *I wish I could go to Paula's flat and talk to her.* Finally, she sat down at the little desk by the window in her room and wrote to Paula. Luisa told her everything about the job and the other nurses. She admitted that she was earning a living, but she was very unhappy. Two weeks later, Luisa squealed with delight when she saw she'd received a letter from Paula.

Dear Luisa,

I am glad you have found work. That takes a little pressure off you, I am sure. I only wish it had been here in Vienna. I hope you understand that I didn't want you to leave my flat, it was just too small for two people. And I am so set in my ways. I am such a creature of habit. I have certain ways of doing things. For instance, I get up very early, and I didn't want to wake you when I had to get ready for work in the morning. When I saw your letter arrive, I was so glad that you had written. I knew that meant that you had forgiven me.

As far as school is concerned, I think it's a wonderful idea for you to return. I know you left high school because of Noam, but you can finish now. Then you can attend nursing school and fulfill your dream. Once you are a nurse, you would always be assured of having a job.

I want you to know that I miss you all the time. I miss our card games and our weekly dinners. But think of it this way, if you were a nurse, you could move back to Vienna. That would be splendid. Perhaps I'll go to nursing school too. Can you just imagine if we were both nurses? How important we would feel. Well, it's late, and I must get some sleep. But please write again soon, and let me know how you're doing.

Your friend, Paula.

Nursing school, Luisa thought. *That would be a dream come true. But hardly possible for a poor girl like me. The only girls who are accepted into nursing school are the rich girls with influential fathers. Not girls whose mothers were maids in Jewish households.*

CHAPTER 10

1918 Spring

The pestilence snuck in quietly at first like a predator in the night. No one realized the magnitude of what was happening.

Slowly, very slowly, a few cases of the flu appeared at the hospital. However, everyone was too overwhelmed with the returning soldiers to take notice. Besides, it was nothing to worry about, they thought; it seemed like little more than the regular seasonal flu. The symptoms were mild, and the illness rarely lasted more than three days. Luisa didn't give it a thought. It seemed like nothing to be alarmed about. And by the time summer came, it was over; there were almost no cases of the flu.

Luisa tried to apply for the *Notabitur*, a test which would qualify her to receive her *Zeugnis der allgemeinen Hochschulreife*, which was a certificate that would allow her to attend nursing school. However, to be approved, she would have to have been evacuated from the city where she lived during the Great War. And since she was not, she would need to take the *Abitur* exam.

Taking Paula's advice, Luisa registered for school. She

knew she would need the extra education if she wanted to pass the exam. Her classes were to begin in the fall, and she was excited to have a plan for her future. She was so excited that she wrote to her mother and told her of her plans. Her mother wrote back telling her that she was glad Luisa was on a better path.

Summer came, and with it came unrelenting heat. And as for Luisa, the summer brought even more unrelenting loneliness. She wished she earned enough money to visit Paula in Vienna. But she had to be satisfied with letters because she hardly made enough to pay her bills. She cursed the son of the restaurant owner in Vienna for ruining her life. If he had not taken over, she figured she would still be living there, where she could see her only friend.

In the stillness of the summer, a time pregnant with possibilities, the disease that would come to be known as the Spanish flu lay quietly watching and waiting, mutating and growing.

It seemed to take forever for the stifling heat to give way to cooler weather. Luisa's small room felt like a sauna, and she found it hard to get much sleep. With a gust of wind and a torrent of leaves, autumn arrived bringing some relief from the heat. Luisa started school. She was not a good student. But she was obedient and sat quietly in the back of the classroom. And because she caused no trouble, the teachers helped her along.

Then it happened, the virus took hold of the city. She gripped it in her fist and shook it to its very core. Hundreds of cases appeared almost overnight. Serious and often fatal cases. And within days, the hospital where Luisa worked was filled with the smell of death. The nurses were terrified of catching the illness.

Everyone was terrified. The school Luisa was attending closed. And Luisa wrote to Paula.

Dear Paula,

I have some bad news and no one here to talk to about it. As I am sure you know, the Spanish flu has caused everyone to panic. The administration closed the school I was attending due to the epidemic. I am so disheartened. It was difficult for me to bring myself to return to school in the first place. I felt so ashamed and singled out entering a classroom at my age. And now, I will have to do it again as soon as this is over. I feel like giving up.

Your friend, Luisa.

Paula wrote back to Luisa:

Dear Luisa,

Don't you dare give up. You must finish high school so you can go on to become a nurse. I have been taking secretarial classes because, although I would love nothing more than to be a nurse, I am afraid I don't have the stomach for it. However, if we both finish school, we could get a job working at the same hospital. We could even rent flats in the same building. Wouldn't that be wonderful? Please don't quit, Luisa. You can do this. I know you can.

Your friend, Paula.

CHAPTER 11

1919

Germany lost the war. The soldiers returned to Germany broken, defeated, and heartsick. With them they brought an even more vicious strain of the flu and another deadly enemy, a need to find a scapegoat. They had to find someone to blame for their shame and loss. And, as it had it been since the beginning of time, that blame fell upon the Jews.

Luisa continued to work at the hospital as the soldiers returned from battle. It seemed like there were endless streams of them, sick, alone, and battle scarred.

The hospital smelled of fear and death. The terror Luisa saw in the eyes of the nurses and the patients reflected the terror she felt in her heart. Then one afternoon after work, she received a telegram from her mother's employer, Noam's mother.

Dear Luisa,

It breaks my heart to have to be the one who tells you this news. Your mother has passed away. She caught that terrible flu. As soon as I knew she was sick, I sent for the finest doctors. I promise you, she had the best care. But I am so sorry, she could not be saved. I would have sent for you, but it all happened so fast, within a few days. Please drop by anytime to pick up your mother's things. I will put them together for you. She had a small savings, which I will put away for you. I want you to know that your mother was more than an employee to us. She was part of our family, and my husband and I loved her. We mourn with you.

Frau Horwitz

Luisa felt sick to her stomach. *My mother is dead. Why? Why was my mother taken so young? I should have gone to see her. I thought about it so many times. But I couldn't go there because of Noam and his wife. The last time I saw her, we were arguing. Now I'll never be able to see her again.*

Luisa thought about how hard her mother had worked to provide for the two of them, and she was suddenly overcome with tenderness. *I was ashamed of her. I was ashamed of our way of living. But I loved her. I did, and now she's gone. If it hadn't been for those Jews she worked for, I would have seen my mother again before she died. But those Jews kept me away from her. They didn't even send word to me that she was dying. I don't believe that lying Jew, Frau Horwitz, that my mother died quickly. She probably didn't even notice that my mother was dying. She was probably too busy with her friends and her social life. I hate the Jews,* Luisa thought. She pounded her pillow and wept. She wept tears of loss mixed with tears of anger.

Although Luisa could have used the money from her mother's savings, she knew she would never return to the Horwitzes' home. She couldn't bear the humiliation of seeing Noam and his wife living there. Luisa remembered the words her mother had often repeated to her when she tried to explain that Noam was different: "The Horwitzes are nice as far as Jews go. But never forget that they are still Jews. And when it comes down to it, they will stick to their own. When it comes time for Noam to marry, he will never marry you. He will marry another Jew like himself."

"Mother . . ." she said aloud as she lay on the small cot alone in her room, "you were right. You worked for them, but you also knew they were our enemies. Frau Horwitz should have sent for me earlier. I should have had an opportunity to say goodbye to you. But she was probably so wrapped up in herself that she didn't know how sick you were. And now you're gone. I hate her and I hate her son. I hate Frau Birnbaum too: Goldie's mother. I hate her for giving me Goldie's old clothes. She did it on purpose. I think she and Goldie made a plan. She would give me the clothes, and then Goldie would use them to humiliate me. Dirty Jews. The Jews are the reason we lost the war. They have ruined our country. And they've ruined my life. Someday I will make them pay. Someday, they'll be sorry for everything they did to me."

Then she sat down and wrote to Paula.

Dear Paula,

My mother died. I feel terrible because I never saw her again after I left her at the Horwitzes' home. Now I will never have the opportunity to speak to her again. If only I could hear her voice one more time. I blame the Jews she worked for. They should have contacted me when she got sick, not after she died. But, of course, since they are Noam's family, I wouldn't expect them to be considerate. Noam was a selfish bastard, just like his mother. He used me. I realize that now. And his parents used my mother to clean their house and cook their food, but when it came down to helping her, they let her die. Mrs. Horwitz said she brought in the best doctors but I don't believe her. She's a Jew. They are liars. Even though my mother and I were not close after I left, I feel as though my heart is bleeding. Every time I close my eyes, I remember something that happened with my mother, like how she comforted me when I was a child. So, I am having trouble sleeping. I can't eat either. If I could find the courage, I would go to see Noam and slap him in the face. But I don't have the courage. I feel so powerless. I wish you were here. I need a friend.

Luisa

Luisa received a reply shortly afterward:

Dear Luisa,

I may not be by your side in Berlin, but I am by your side in my heart. When I read your letter, I wept for you. I know how terrible you must feel. I wish I had the money to come and see you. I am lonely here too. And you're right, it is the fault of those Jews. They should have gotten in touch with you right away. I don't believe for a minute that it happened quickly, and they had no time. I think you're right; they just didn't care. And I am so sorry for you.

Paula

CHAPTER 12

1921

Luisa was working on an assembly line in a factory again. These jobs were difficult for women to get since the men had returned from the war needing work. Most of the companies tried to hire men with families now. Meanwhile, the women who had worked this job during the war had since returned home to their husbands and families.

When Luisa went into the factory to ask for a job, the man who interviewed her was a fatherly type. She could see in his eyes that he felt sorry for her when she told him she was on her own. She explained that she had to support herself because she was unmarried. "I have no family or husband to turn to," she'd told him honestly. He'd looked her over and with sad eyes; he'd shaken his head and offered her the position.

The job wasn't hard once she learned how to work her machine. It was almost robotic. As was always the case, she had no friends at work. This time, however, there were fewer women. Some of the men made lewd suggestions to her, but she ignored them. They were married and looking for trouble.

She was not. It wasn't because she hadn't had her share of one-night stands. She'd had plenty. But she was tired of being the subject of everyone's ridicule at the workplace. She was getting older and learning to keep to herself. This time, at this job, she wanted to be left alone.

After she finished her shift one summer afternoon, she walked to the corner deli to buy some salami. It was a luxury for her. Luisa told herself that she had been working hard and knew she deserved it. This was a Jewish deli, and she hated to give them her business. However, she had never forgotten the taste of kosher salami from when she'd lived at the Horwitzes' home, and sometimes she craved it.

"Good afternoon, young lady." A Jewish man wearing a skull cap, stood behind the counter.

"I would like four slices of salami," she said. Luisa had come here before, and the man was always kind to her.

"Of course." He smiled, taking the salami and putting it on a large wood block. Then he began to cut it with a sharp knife. He looked at her in her worn dress with her sad eyes and cut two extra slices. Then he wrapped it all in paper. "Enjoy," he said.

"What is the price now?" she asked, knowing that the hyperinflation was making money almost worthless.

"What do you have?" he asked.

"Not much," she said, shaking her head. "I can hardly afford to pay my rent. Every time I try to buy something to eat, the price has gone up. I can't shop in the morning when the housewives shop because I have to work. And by the time I finish my shift, I can't afford to buy a loaf of bread because the price has risen so high during the day.

"Ehh, I know. This hyperinflation is killing everyone," he said. "How about this? Today, it's on me."

"That's very kind of you."

"Don't mention it. We all have to help each other. That's what makes the world go around, no?"

Luisa nodded. "Thank you." She took the package and left.

When she arrived back at home, a letter was waiting for her. She grabbed the letter, excited to see Paula's handwriting. Then she ran upstairs to eat her dinner and read her letter.

Dear Luisa,

I have such news!!! You won't believe it. I had a visitor. My brother, Adalwolf, came to see me. I haven't seen him in an awfully long time. When I saw his face, it was like he was an angel who had fallen from heaven. He looks so strong and handsome. He told me that he had served in the war and that he was a hero! I didn't even know he was in the service, but I was so proud to hear it. Then he told me that he has recently become the leader of the National Socialist German Worker's Party. He suggested that I look into joining. Perhaps you would like to join as well. He said there are divisions of it in Germany as well as here in Austria. Everything he told me about it sounds wonderful!!!!! Look into it if you can. And keep your eyes open for his name in the newspapers. He is becoming an important man. But you won't find him under Adalwolf. That's just my pet name for him. His real name is Adolf. And our real last name is not Wolff, it's Hitler. So, look for him; his name is Adolf Hitler. Yes, Hitler is my real surname too. Wolff is just a name I am using. Anyway, remember my brother, Adolf. You mark my words, I just know he is going to go far in this world.

Your friend, Paula.

Luisa smiled and folded the letter. She missed Paula.

After an exhausting and horrifying period, the flu epidemic finally began to subside. There were fewer and fewer cases. However, the fear still lingered. But now, with hyperinflation, people were starving. Every day, in fact, every hour, the German mark was worth less and less. Luisa had hardly earned enough money to survive before this set in, and with hyperinflation, her meager salary hardly sufficed. The lines for bread were long. The housewives got in line for flour or bread early in the morning because by the end of the day the bread was either gone or too expensive to buy. The money was becoming worthless. Luisa bartered for food: cleaning houses, doing wash, mending clothing, babysitting, and anything else she could find to supplement her income.

One afternoon, on her day off, as Luisa was waiting in line for flour, she saw a man standing across the street handing out leaflets. He was speaking loudly, and the crowd was listening.

"It's the Jews who got us into this mess. They are the reason we lost the war. And make no mistake, as you stand in that line with your suitcases filled with worthless money, you should know that it is the Jewish bankers that are taking the food out of the mouths of your babies. Pay attention! The time is now! Fellow Germans, we must take back what is rightfully ours. If you ignore this warning, the tricky Jews will steal everything you own. Come to our meeting tonight. There is much you should learn."

Luisa was touched by his words. They struck a nerve inside her. She had been waiting for something like this . . . for someone to blame for all she'd been through . . . for someone to punish . . . for someone to change the shape of Germany. *Haven't I seen the selfishness of the greedy Jews firsthand? Didn't Noam take advantage of me? Didn't his mother take advantage of my mother? And what about Frau Birnbaum. She gave me those dresses so her daughter could publicly humiliate me. They were all Jews.*

Luisa stepped out of line. This was more important to her than buying bread. She walked over to the man and took a pamphlet. "I'll be there tonight," she declared.

The man nodded and smiled at her.

Luisa put on her nicest dress and attended the meeting that night. When she arrived, she was pleasantly surprised to discover it was a meeting of the National Socialist German

Workers Party. She remembered Paula writing to her and telling her that her brother, Adolf, was the leader of this group.

Proudly, Luisa told the others at the meeting about her friendship with Paula. She explained that Paula was Adolf's younger sister. They welcomed Luisa with open arms. Luisa felt wanted, like she was a part of something and not just an outsider looking in, although she was not permitted to join the party, as only men were permitted to become members. As a woman, she was allowed to march in their demonstrations and join several of their organizations that had been created for women. Luisa felt at home. She felt she belonged with these people.

CHAPTER 13

1924

Dear Luisa,

I have terrible news!

My brother has been arrested in Munich. His friend telephoned me last night to let me know. He said that my brother was very depressed. He was even contemplating suicide. I wish I could have been there so I could show him how much he means to me. But he never contacted me, so I never even knew he was in a bad way. His friend said Adolf had been hiding in an attic for two days. And now, from what his friend says, my brother is being tried for treason. I am sick with worry, but I don't have enough money to go to him so I must wait for news. I am not quite sure what he did exactly. His friend's letter wasn't clear. What I do know is that his arrest had something to do with an attempt to seize power by kidnapping some politicians. It happened last year. So, I don't know why he is being arrested now. And I don't know what is going to happen to him. But I am very distraught.

Yours, Paula

Luisa read the letter and felt her face grow hot. *She's right, this is terrible news. I don't know what to say to her. But I must write to her right away so she knows she is in my thoughts.*

Luisa picked up a pen and paper and began to write.

Dear Paula,

I was shocked when I read your letter. I hope all will work out for you and your brother. I don't know what else to say. Please write and let me know what happens.

By the way, I've taken your advice. I haven't given up on my education. I started back to school.

Your friend, Luisa.

47

CHAPTER 14

1924 The Beginning of March

Luisa came home from school to find a letter from Paula. She knew from the newspapers that Adolf Hitler was in a lot of trouble. She hadn't written to Paula because she didn't know what to say to her. In fact, even now, she was afraid to open the letter, afraid of what it would say. She took out a pen and paper and began to do her homework. But she couldn't concentrate. Paula was on her mind. So she read the letter.

Dear Luisa,

I have not seen or heard from Adolf. But I have been following my brother's trial. It has been all over the newspapers here. I am sure it has been in the papers there too. I've been on edge every day. And yesterday I am sorry to say that I found out that Adolf has been sentenced to five years in Landsberg Prison. I can't imagine him imprisoned. I do hope he will be all right. They don't know him the way I do. He's always been a sensitive sort, an artist. I am afraid that his imprisonment will kill him.

Your friend, Paula.

Luisa felt sick to her stomach. She'd never been good at comforting anyone else. But she felt certain that Paula was waiting for a response. And she didn't want to keep her waiting. So she wrote a letter full of encouragement. This was the best she felt she could do for her friend.

Dear Paula,

Your brother's trial has been all over the papers here as well. They are publishing every one of his defense speeches. And I must say, you should be very proud, because he is quite impressive when he speaks. When I attend party meetings, it is the general consensus that the fact Adolf is receiving a lot of publicity is good for our cause. And although it is unfortunate that he's been arrested, it seems that more and more people are joining our movement because of the newspapers. And so, it might not turn out as badly as you think. However, I, too, worry for his safety in prison. There is nothing we can do right now. All we can do is stay hopeful that things will turn out well.

Luisa

CHAPTER 15

Luisa had stolen a bottle of schnapps and was having a drink in her room as she read Paula's latest letter.

Dear Luisa,

My brother has been released from prison. I was so worried about him, but he only ended up serving eighteen months. How wonderful is that? Good news, yes?

I was afraid for Adolf when he was in prison. But it seems he has done quite well. Wait until you hear this: Adolf has written a book!!!! He wouldn't want me to say this to anyone, but, of course, you are like a sister to me, so I'll tell you. Adolf was never much of an intellectual. So, it is rather strange that he wrote a book. He was always more of an artist. However, the poor fellow never had much luck with art either. So, I am assuming he may well have changed his career focus to a more intellectual and political path. I know this may sound strange, but, in my heart, I believe my brother has a destiny to fulfill and that somehow, he will change the world.

Meanwhile, as for me, I went on a date with a nice man. But so far, I haven't heard from him. I wait each day, but he doesn't drop by or call. I'll keep you abreast of everything that happens.

Your friend,

Paula.

Luisa had never had much luck with men. She'd had plenty of one-night stands during her lifetime. After Noam, she met plenty of boys, and then men as she grew older, who spent passionate nights with her. They were always promising to drop by as they hurried out the door in the morning. But they never did. The first few men after Noam hurt her when they didn't come to call. She wanted to be important to someone, to be a wife, and mother. Every time she took a man to her bed, she hoped he might be a potential husband and father for her children, even if he was just a man she met an hour or two before in a restaurant or tavern. When she was younger, she wept and felt alone and abandoned. But as the years passed, she began to expect that marriage was not in her future, and she began to accept that sex was just sex, nothing more. The tears stopped, and instead she set her sights on finishing school and learning a trade.

The more Luisa was around the nurses at the hospital, the more certain she was that she wanted to be a nurse. However, it was difficult to see that far into the future. Right now, she was working long hours, and it was taking her longer than she expected to finish school. Sometimes she felt overwhelmed and disheartened. But there was no one to fall back on, no one to help her. So she pushed along through school with a hovering dream of being accepted by a group of other nurses and being respected and admired by doctors and patients.

One afternoon, Luisa was surprised to see a package wrapped in brown paper arrive in the mail for her. She'd never received a gift through the mail. And she couldn't imagine who would have sent it. Paula was her only friend, and she knew Paula did not have money for gifts. Carefully, she removed the paper and put it down on the desk. Later she would fold it and put it into a drawer where she would save it in case she might need it in the future. Inside the package was a book. She read the title, which said, *Mein Kampf* (My Struggle) in heavy black letters. Then she read the note. It was from Paula:

I hope you enjoy my brother's book. It was very enlightening for me.

CHAPTER 16

Luisa read the book. Every word seemed to speak directly to her. She agreed that Germany must colonize Eastern Europe, and it must also make sure to take control of Russia. She began to secretly refer to Paula's brother as Adalwolf in her own mind. The more she read, the closer she felt to him. And she began to daydream that someday they might meet, and he might just be the man she'd been waiting for. It was only a fantasy, and she knew that, but the very thought made her feel giddy. As Luisa read Adolf's words explaining that the Jews must be eliminated from Germany because they had caused all of Germany's problems, she said "Yes" aloud. A smile came over her face. Then she wrote to Paula.

Dear Paula,

I am enthralled with the book. I have been reading it every free moment that I have. It is truly wonderful. You were right, it is filled with insight. I hope someday I will have the opportunity to meet your brother. What a special fellow he must be.

Luisa

She sealed the letter and mailed it. That night she dreamed of Adalwolf.

Soon after, Paula's latest letter came.

Dear Luisa,

I'm so glad you're enjoying the book. My brother is a very special person. He has many talents. I know I told you that he wanted to be an artist, but the war changed his mind. I believe he changed his mind because he knew that Germany needed him. He is like that. Only a truly remarkable man would give up his own dreams to save his country. I do hope the day comes when you two will meet. But I can't say when that might happen. I hardly see him myself. I do wish he would come by or write more. But that's Adalwolf. He's busy, but I know he loves me. After all, he is my brother.

By the way, that boy I met, the one I told you about. He never telephoned. I don't know why. But I was disappointed. I'm getting older. I would like to marry and have children someday. However, I don't know when that might happen, so for now I am enjoying secretarial work. I think it may be a good career choice for me.

Yours, Paula.

CHAPTER 17

1929

Dear Paula,

The German Worker's Party was involved in a demonstration today. And you won't believe this, but I was leading a group of young girls in the demonstration when I saw a face right out of my past. Do you remember me telling you about Goldie Birnbaum? Well, in case you forgot, she made my years in high school miserable. I was so terrified of her as a teenager that I hid and never fought back when she tormented me. But when I saw her in the street and I was surrounded by people who shared my values, I felt so brave. I walked right up to her and called her a dirty Jew, which she is. Then do you know what I did? I kicked her right in her ass. Do you know what inspired me to do that? It was your brother's book. He gave me the self-confidence I needed. Anyway, you should have seen her face. She was appalled. But I felt good. I felt powerful and for the first time, I didn't feel like she was better than me. I wanted to share this with you, because Goldie, and all the Jews in that neighborhood where I grew up thought I was dirt. And now we, the Germans, are rising. Like Adalwolf said, we will soon be in power and then we will pay them back for all they've done.

Your friend always,

Luisa

Dear Luisa,

If I remember correctly, Goldie's mother was the one who gave you all the expensive dresses, and then Goldie humiliated you by telling all the other students that they were her old clothes. Well, she got what she deserved didn't she? You're correct when you say the Germanic people are rising. My brother did tell of this in his book, and I am so glad that I am living in this very important time in history. I told you that Adalwolf was a special person. Now, I am beginning to think he might even be a genius.

Your friend, Paula

CHAPTER 18

1933

Luisa had never received a telegram from Paula before. She'd always written letters. So, when the telegram arrived, Luisa's heart skipped a beat. She was worried. What would make Paula pay to send her note? Her hands trembled as she opened the telegram.

Dear Luisa,

My brother has been appointed chancellor of Germany! I feel the winds of destiny changing for our family. The Hitlers are going to be remembered throughout history. I am so excited I can hardly eat or sleep.

Your friend, Paula.

Dear Paula,

I am so happy for you. You should be so proud. Your brother is an important man.

I have some good news too. Finally, after a long and

difficult time, I've finished school. Finally. It's been hard, but I have a diploma. I am still working long hours as a cleaning woman at the hospital, but I have started nursing school. They've finally opened it up to everyone. It used to be that only wealthy girls from prominent families were permitted to become nurses. But now, everyone can become a nurse. It finally feels like my dream is possible. After all, Hendrich Himmler's wife is a nurse. Did you know that? It is such an honor to embark on such a worthy career. And from what I read in your brother's book, nurses are going to be needed in the East when the fatherland begins to colonize the savages there. I want so much to be a contributing part of the new Germany. The Germany your brother will create. A land that will restore us to our rightful place of power in the world.

I, too, feel the winds of change. Soon the Jews will be powerless, and we, the Aryans will take over the world like an army of Teutonic knights. And you and I, Aryan women, will be an important part of changes that are to come.

Your friend always, Luisa.

Luisa went out for a few minutes to mail the letter. When she returned, she sat in the chair in her room and looked at the copy of *Mein Kampf* Paula had sent. She'd finished the book. And she was excited to have found a place for herself in nursing. But she also knew that nurses should be caring and compassionate, and she wasn't. In fact, she didn't care for the well-being of others at all. For her, this career meant acceptance and admiration and, maybe if she was lucky, a little power.

CHAPTER 19

1939 Spring

Luisa had just completed nursing school. Her heart swelled with pride. She wasn't a good student, and it had been harder for her than some of the other girls. But she'd persevered, and now she was graduating. During her training she'd formed a friendship with one of her instructors. This woman had once been a nurse but had traded the difficult job of working with patients for a teaching position. She saw how Luisa struggled, and she went out of her way to help. The instructor had received information about a new program that would be hiring nurses. After the graduation ceremony, she went to speak to Luisa about it. The other graduating nurses were standing with friends and family. She found Luisa standing in the corner alone.

"Congratulations," she said, smiling. "I knew you could do it."

Luisa smiled brightly. "You helped me so much. Thank you."

"But of course. And I have some rather interesting news to share with you. I've received a letter from the government about a program. It seems they are in search of nurses. From what I understand they will be paying well. Better pay than a regular hospital. I'm afraid that is all I know about the job. The letter did state that this is top secret. But what isn't these days? The truth is, it sounds exciting. If I were a younger woman, I would go and apply. Are you interested?"

"Oh yes, I certainly am."

"Well then, take this," her instructor said, handing Luisa a sheet of paper. "Here is all the information I have about the job."

"Thank you, Frau Weib. I will look into it."

"I know I would look into it. I mean, why not, right? The more money you can earn, the better, yes?"

"Yes," Luisa agreed. She and her instructor had several conversations over the course of Luisa's studies. Luisa knew that her instructor had come from a poor family and that she'd grown up with just her mother. There was a small differ- ence: Luisa's father had left them. Her instructor's father had died. But still, both of their mothers had to find ways to support their children on their own. The similarity in their backgrounds was the basis for their friendship.

The day after graduation, Luisa took her instructor's advice. She took a bath and washed her hair. Then she dressed in her best skirt and blouse and boarded a bus to Tier- gartenstrabe 4, where she got off. It was a short walk to the Chancellery Department where the interviews were being held. *What if they don't like me?* she thought as she walked inside. And suddenly she wanted to leave. All the time she'd spent in school could not get rid of the insecurities she was feeling. *Is everyone looking at me? Do they think my clothes are too old and worn? I've come this far. I can't turn back now. I must see this through.* Her knees were weak, but she forced herself to walk up to a woman who was sitting at the front desk.

Luisa stood tall and cleared her throat, then she said, "Heil Hitler!"

"Heil Hitler!" the young woman answered.

Luisa stammered, "Good afternoon. My name is Luisa Eisenreich. I am a nurse." A smile came to Luisa's face when she said those words. *I am a nurse! It is true. After all the work and education, I am finally a real nurse.*

"Ahh, I see. Then you must be here to speak to our recruiter?"

"Yes, I am. Frau Weib was my instructor at nursing school. She sent me here."

"Very good. Please have a seat, Fräulein Eisenreich. Someone will be right with you."

It was less than ten minutes before a tall, strong-looking woman, with ice-blonde hair that was perfectly waved, walked out of one of the offices. She headed directly for Luisa as if there were something in Luisa's face that told her it was Luisa who had come for the interview.

"Fräulein Eisenreich?" she said as she approached.

Luisa stood up. "Yes. I am Luisa Eisenreich."

"Heil Hitler!" the woman said, saluting.

"Heil Hitler!" Luisa saluted.

The woman smiled. "Won't you follow me, please?"

They walked into a functioning, but not fancy, room. There was a well-used wooden desk with a chair behind it and two in front for visitors. A picture of the führer hung on the wall.

The interview was grueling. The woman behind the desk tapped her pencil as she asked Luisa what seemed like a million personal questions. She did not offer Luisa any encouragement. She was not friendly, and she didn't look Luisa in the eyes. Instead, she took notes as they spoke. The woman was almost robotic in her way of speaking. She wanted to know everything about Luisa, including very personal things. The woman asked where Luisa was born and what her parents did for a living. Luisa was ashamed to admit that her father had abandoned her mother leaving her mother penniless and forcing her to take a job as a maid for a Jewish family. "My mother and I lived in the maid's quarters in the home of those Jews," she said.

"How did you feel about that? How did you feel about those Jews?"

"I hated them. I hated them for everything that they took from the good German people."

The woman nodded, revealing nothing. Then she asked, "How do you feel about the sick, or the mentally incompetent, or the weak? In other words, what are your feelings about the useless eaters. The shirkers who take more from our society than they give."

"I hate them. They, like the Jews and other subhumans, are destroying our fatherland."

"Yes, they are," the woman said, revealing the first bit of personal information since the interview began. Then she looked up from her notes into Luisa's eyes and added, "Now, tell me about the jobs you've held in the past and why you are no longer there."

"Oh, well, I've had several without much luck," Luisa stammered. She hesitated, then she added, "I did live in Vienna for a while where I had a very good job working as a waitress in a restaurant. But the owner got too old to keep up the restaurant and he gave it to his son. His son fired me so he could give his wife my job. It doesn't matter, though, because I never really wanted to be a waitress. I've always wanted to be a nurse. And now, I have my license."

"I see. Now, tell me about your friends. Do you have any friends who are Jews, or Gypsies?"

"Of course not. In fact, my best friend is Paula Hitler, our chancellor's younger sister."

"Hmmm." The woman wrote that down in her notes, then asked, "And, if that is so, then why have you not asked her for help in finding you suitable work?"

"She is living in Vienna. I don't have the money to move

there right now. When I decided to go to nursing school, I did it because I was hoping I could find work on my own merit."

"I see," the interviewer said. Then she leaned back in her chair and lit a cigarette. She smiled at Luisa, then she said apologetically, "I know the führer does not approve of women smoking, and I am trying to quit."

Luisa didn't answer because she didn't know what to say.

"Do you smoke?"

"Sometimes," Luisa admitted, "but I can't really afford it."

By the time the woman closed her book and put down her pencil, Luisa was convinced she had not been chosen for employment in the program. The woman stood up and thanked her for the interview.

"Heil Hitler!" the woman said.

Luisa, knowing the interview was over, stood up and answered, "Heil Hitler!" Then she left the woman's office feeling dejected. She slowly walked back to the bus stop and waited until the bus arrived that took her back to her room at the boarding house. *I wish I were still living in Vienna. Paula couldn't help me find work when I lived there. But maybe that was because her brother had not even entered the government yet. Perhaps Paula could help me now. But how can I get the money to move?*

She locked the door to her small room and then sat down at the desk and ate two boiled potatoes for dinner. After she'd finished, she changed into her nightdress and lay down to sleep on her cot. Luisa was exhausted, but she still wished she had a bottle of Göring-Schnaps. It would take the edge off the depression she was feeling. It was not late; in fact, the sun had not yet set. But sleeping was better than sitting alone in her room. Shrugging, she closed her eyes to try to sleep. As she began to drift off, there was a knock on the door to her room.

"Luisa . . ."

"Yes," she answered sleepily.

"There's a phone call for you."

Luisa never received phone calls except from Paula who

called once a year on her birthday. She was worried that something had happened to Paula. She grabbed her robe and tossed it on as ran down the hall to the phone.

"Hello," she said.

"Is this Luisa Eisenreich?"

"Yes." Luisa was trembling. *Who could be calling me? I hope nothing has happened to Paula.*

"This is Frau Zimmer. I'm calling to let you know that you have been hired."

Hired? I hardly expected this. I can't believe it, I got the job! Luisa almost jumped in the air, she was so excited. "Thank you, thank you so much," she said.

"Report to the Chancellery Department tomorrow morning at eight. You will be given further instructions when you arrive."

"I'll be there."

Suddenly Luisa had a burst of energy. She took a shower and set her hair in pin curls. Then she picked up her skirt and blouse from the floor where she'd thrown them when she got home earlier and hung them up. "I got the job. I am a nurse," she said aloud and smiled.

CHAPTER 20

Very early in the morning, Luisa's alarm clock sounded. But she was already awake, too excited to sleep. Luisa got out of bed. She washed her face and hands and then took the pin curls out of her hair. Pausing for a moment, she looked in the mirror. *I wish I were prettier. I wish I were one of those tall girls with perfect blonde hair.* Luisa sighed. She studied her reflection. With her deeply lined brow and thin lips, she looked dark and brooding. Life had made her eyes angry and hard.

And although she wasn't fat, her figure was just ordinary. *There is nothing special about me. My breasts and hips are small. It would probably be easier to find a husband if my hips were wider. Men want a woman who looks like she could easily bear a child.* Luisa ran her hands down the front of her slip. *And I am not athletic either. If only I were beautiful. My life might have been different if I were a beauty. Perhaps Noam would have married me*, she thought. *There I go wishing again.* Then she reminded herself, *Wishing hasn't changed things for me yet.* Letting out a loud sigh, she picked up her clothes and put them on. She still owned a pair of silk stockings that she'd stolen from Noam's mother when she lived at his home but they had a run in them, so she decided against wearing them.

Then she ran a comb through her hair, grabbed her hand-bag, and left her room. She was on her way, headed for the chancellery. The bus was on time and she took that as a good sign. *I think things are going to start going my way.*

When she arrived at the chancellery, she was led into a large room where twenty other women were gathered. They all sat quietly and waited. Then a young pretty blonde, tall and slender, who looked like she would be a wonderful athlete, walked into the room. She had a natural blush, almost a glow to her cheeks, and her lips were just slightly red. Luisa was immediately envious of her.

"Heil Hitler!" she said to the group of women.

"Heil Hitler!" the women answered in unison.

"It's a lovely morning isn't it, Fräuleins?" she said, smiling.

"Yes," they answered.

"I'd like to introduce myself. I'm Thelka Vogel, and I am very pleased to see all of you looking so well and eager this morning." She smiled, and Luisa thought she was incredibly beautiful. Then she went on to say, "Each of you has been carefully chosen for this job. I cannot express to you how important this position is. You will be carrying out a top-secret mission for our fatherland. Can you keep a secret?" she said conspiratorially.

"Yes," the girls all said.

"Good. Because this is a very, very secret mission. And . . . as I said, an important one. Now, do you recall when you were in school and you were in your mathematics class? I'll bet at some point you must have been asked to calculate how large of an expense the disabled are in our country. Once you finished putting the numbers together, you were probably shocked to see how much of a burden these poor souls are and have always been on the fatherland." The pretty young woman stopped speaking and hesitated for a moment. She looked around the room, making eye contact with each of the girls.

Then she continued. "By now, I am sure you know that I am speaking of the useless eaters. The unfortunates who live worthless lives. They are either mentally or physically defective. And because of this, they never make any sort of contribution to society. Instead, they spend their entire lives taking from our government. If we allow them to, they will take and take until they have sucked all of our resources dry. This will greatly weaken the fatherland."

Luisa nodded her head. She'd studied that very subject intensely, and she realized that whatever mission this was, it was very important that the useless eaters be dealt with as soon as possible.

"Now," Thelka Vogel said, "sometimes, when you are in the process of rebuilding a country, a country you know has greatness within, like our precious fatherland, it may be necessary to do things that are distasteful. Yet . . ." And again, she hesitated, "these things must be done for the good of the country. Do you understand me?"

Luisa nodded. She was no longer looking around to see what the other women were doing. Her eyes were glued to the speaker. She agreed with every word.

"Do you want to see Germany restored to her rightful place of greatness?"

"Yes!" the women shouted.

"Do you want it more than anything else in the world?"

"Yes!" they said again.

"Are you willing to do whatever must be done in order to achieve that end?"

"Yes!"

"Good!"

CHAPTER 21

Luisa was given two weeks to prepare to leave Berlin and move to a town called Hadamar. But because the woman's speech had encouraged her so much, she went home and began to make arrangements to leave that same day. She called the hospital and gave notice that she was planning to leave in two weeks. Then she began to sort through her things. *I've never heard of Hadamar before. But I am excited to start a new life there. I am now a nurse, no longer the cleaning woman. And I am thrilled to be doing such important work,* she thought as she placed a few of her possessions into a small valise. Luisa didn't have much, but she packed everything that was nonessential—pictures, letters from Paula and her mother. Her copy of *Mein Kampf. I will pack the rest right before I go. I am ready to leave Berlin. I just know that this new life is going to be better. Fräulein Vogel said that I would receive room and board as well as a good salary. And she even said that the fresh country air in Hadamar will be good for my health. Perhaps after living in the country for a while, I'll be as pretty as she is,* Luisa mused.

The two weeks passed slowly. Every day, she went into work and cleaned the dirty rooms, the vomit, the feces, the urine. She would have liked to quit, but she thought it was best to work and save every penny right until the time she left.

Finally, the day arrived. Her toes tingled as she boarded the train. *I am on my way,* she thought. As the train pulled out of the station, Luisa took a pen and paper from her handbag and wrote to Paula, sending her the new address where she would be staying, and telling her about her new position.

The train ride to Hadamar took over six hours, with the train making several stops along the way. But once they were out of the city, Luisa was enchanted. It was early morning, and there was a light mist of dew on the grass and flowers. She hummed softly to herself as she marveled at the beauty of the German countryside. *Everything is so green,* she thought. *And so lovely.* Tiny buds had begun to form on the trees. *I've never been in the country before. It's strange to see so much open space.*

When the train stopped in Hadamar, Luisa got off. It was a small village. When she asked directions from an old woman, who was selling strawberries, the old woman gave her a toothless smile and pointed. "I know just where you are going," she said, then added, "The House of Shutters isn't a far walk. But what's a girl like you going to the crazy house for? Are they trying to put you in there? Or are you visiting a relative?"

"Oh no, it's nothing like that at all," Luisa said. "I'm a nurse."

The old woman nodded her head. "A nurse," she said, impressed. "If I was a nurse, I wouldn't work there. I'm scared of crazy people. So, I stay far away from that place." Then she grabbed a few strawberries from her basket, and with a wrinkled hand she gave them to Luisa. "Take these, they're very sweet. And by the way, good luck to you."

"Thank you," Luisa said. The strawberries were indeed sweet. Luisa ate them as she walked toward the institute. *A crazy house? The old woman called it a crazy house. What she means is a mental hospital. What am I going to be doing at a mental hospital?* As Luisa walked along, she remembered what Fräulein Vogel had said and suddenly it became clear to her. She had a good idea of what was going to be expected of her. It gave her chills. But she knew that this task she would be completing must be done in order to help the fatherland. Even so, it was sordid business, and she hoped she would be able to do it.

When Luisa arrived at the Hadamar Institute, she was shown to her a room. It was a bright and cheery room which she shared with three other girls who were younger than herself. The girls were mostly in their twenties, while Luisa had just turned forty-two. Once again, she was an outsider. The others had not been at the institute long, but they'd already formed friendships. Luisa had hoped that things would be different this time. But they weren't. She had that same old feeling of being left out. Luisa wanted to make friends, but she wasn't sure how to do it. So she kept to herself. That first night after she arrived, she went to dinner. No one invited her to eat with them. She found a seat alone at the end of the long table and listened to the other girls talking about the recent outings they shared on their days off.

The following morning, Luisa was directed to a lecture hall where her job was explained to her in detail. As she listened, she shook her head. The job was just what she expected. *It will be hard to do, but I am doing my part. My work is an important part of the efforts to clean up the fatherland.*

"Sometimes your work may be difficult because, after all, these poor souls are not shirkers. They are not lazy; they just can't help themselves. By euthanizing them, you are doing them a favor. You are helping them to leave their useless, unproductive existence behind, and at the same time you are cleansing the fatherland of worthless baggage that is draining our economy," the nurse in charge explained to the new hires.

"How must we do it?" a young girl in the front row asked.

"It will all be in a very humane way. They won't suffer at all."

By the time the lecture was over, the girls were enthusiastic

about their importance. They were about to take their place in
the building of the new Germany.

CHAPTER 22

Luisa was told to watch a few of the procedures before she was expected to carry out her first one. The patients were to be kept calm. They were spoken to in a soft and gentle voice. Then they were told they were being given something to help them feel calm and get some sleep. Once the patient was asleep, a doctor would do a quick examination and give his approval for the patient to be euthanized. The nurse would then administer the injection. And within minutes it was over. Once the patient was dead, the doctors would dissect the corpses for use in medical experimentation.

The first patient Luisa euthanized was a young man who had to be restrained to the bed because of violent outbursts. He screamed out obscenities and called Luisa names. He was so resistant and fighting so hard that the needle broke when she tried to give him the injection that would calm him and put him to sleep. "What should I do now?" she asked her trainer.

"Give him the other injection," the trainer said. But the man would not lie still. "Wait a moment." The trainer left the room. She returned a few minutes later with three doctors who restrained the man. He cursed and cried out. The other patients in the other rooms on the floor became agitated. They, too, started to scream. "Hurry up. This man is causing havoc here," one of the doctors said.

Luisa's hands shook as she inserted the needle into the man's arm. "Bitch," he said. She trembled. Within seconds, he was quiet. She placed the syringe on a white cloth on a table next to the bed and walked out of the room. Still trembling, she went to the lunchroom and plopped down. Luisa was breathing heavily. Her heart was racing. *A man died at my hands today. I killed a man. I know it was for the good of our country, but I am unnerved. I wish I had a drink or something to calm me.*

She sat for a long while. No one came to find her or to talk to her. And she didn't feel comfortable enough about what she'd done to write about it to Paula. Besides, she'd vowed never to tell anyone what was being done at the institute. So she had to bear this alone. Luisa shivered as she tried not to think about the face of the man whom she'd just euthanized. *They should have tied him to the bed. He was wild.* Evidence of his madness had been written all over his contorted face. She tried not to hear his wild and terrifying screams and curses. *I helped to quiet him. He was so peaceful after the injection.*

Then she reminded herself of all the things this job was offering her, a nice, clean place to live, a good salary, and a purpose. *I am serving the fatherland. The women I work with here at the institute have the same goals I do, to see Germany restored to her rightful place in the world. Perhaps I have finally found a home for myself. Perhaps as time goes by I will find friends here at the Hadamar Institute and finally be accepted as a part of something bigger than myself. That is all I have ever really wanted. That and to be loved. It might be too late for me to find love, but if I speak out to the others about my devotion to the party, maybe, just maybe, I will find friends.* Luisa got up and straightened her uniform. *As they say, the first time is always the most difficult. I've gotten that out of the way now. And I am ready to do what must be done,* she thought.

By the end of the following week, Luisa had administered

more than twenty syringes bringing death. Each time, she told herself that she was peacefully ended the suffering of a useless eater.

One afternoon, an hour after lunch, Luisa was called in to be available for questions to a group of students who a teacher had brought into the institute.

"Don't mention the injections," Luisa's superior said. "Just watch and listen. If they ask you anything, be vague in your answers."

Luisa nodded.

The teacher was a young, tall, slender, red-haired woman. She wore no cosmetics. Luisa knew the Reich was against the wearing of makeup, but in secret she still loved to apply just a touch of lipstick to her cheeks and lips. For years she'd been so careful to sparingly use the tube she'd stolen. It was saved for the most special occasions. But now, since she was earning money, she was able to purchase a new tube of bright red lipstick. And she used just a smidgen every day.

"You see these patients in here?" the young teacher said to her class. "They are all useless eaters. They can't help it, but they are destroying our government. Fortunately, our führer has found a way to control them by sending them to homes like these where they are given the bare minimum so as not to set us back. We are trying to rebuild our fatherland."

One young girl raised her hand. "I am afraid of them. Their bodies are twisted, and they scream and cry."

"And well you should be afraid of them. They are dangerous. However, that is not why you were brought here. You were not brought here to be frightened. I brought you here to Hadamar to remind you of your own superiority. Look at these poor souls. They hardly have a right to exist. They offer nothing to the world. They just take. We work hard, and the money we spend to keep them alive is a waste of our resources. You"—the young teacher pointed to the students in her class—"you are the future of our fatherland. The pride of our führer. You are pure Aryans, the finest of all races. Born to lead. Born to take power."

That night when Luisa went back to her room, she remembered the young teacher's words. *I am pure Aryan*, she thought. *I am the pride of the fatherland.*

CHAPTER 23

It became easier to administer the injections, routine almost. And as time passed, Luisa began to enjoy the sensation of power. When she walked into the room, the patient would not live to see another day. She, Luisa, the girl who had always been powerless, held that much power in her hands. It gave her a heady feeling. The depression she'd lived with for years seemed to lift, and with it, her personal hygiene improved. Each night she showered and set her hair in pin curls. Her uniform was clean and pressed. This was all new for Luisa. She was now an important person, a person with a purpose and a very vital job to carry out. She walked with her head held high. No longer did she keep her head down avoiding the gaze of others. Instead, she began to look the other nurses in the eye and say "Heil Hitler!" each morning as she picked up her daily assignment at the nurses' desk.

It was exciting to her that the patients who she was about to euthanize had no idea what was in store for them. They had already been given something to calm them when Luisa entered the room with a smile. She would call them by name, and her very presence exuded confidence, so they trusted her as she slipped the needle into their arms. "This won't hurt a bit," she would say with a smile, then she'd add, "And it will make you feel good. It will help you to calm down." Most of the patients didn't give her any trouble; they would lie still and allow her to administer the injection.

On the rare occasion when a patient fought her and had to be restrained, she would become angry. Once it took several people to tie a female patient securely to the bed. Luisa let her internal rage surface. She leaned down and whispered in the woman's ear, "You are about to die. I am about to murder you." The patient let out a scream. This enraged Luisa even more. She held the syringe in front of the woman's face. The woman struggled to break free of the ties that bound her, but she wasn't strong enough. Luisa said, "You have given me a lot of trouble this morning. So now you deserve to suffer."

Over the next several months, Luisa made friends. She went out of her way to befriend the other nurses as well as the doctors who she worked with. And she was thrilled when she was invited to join the other nurses when they all went out together on the weekends. They alternated days off, but whenever she was able to attend an outing, she did. The nurses who spent their workdays euthanizing the helpless, spent their days off taking hikes and going on picnics. One of the girls had a camera, and she took pictures of the smiling nurses.

Luisa was careful to keep her friends. She laughed when they made jokes or did imitations of Irmgard Huber, the head nurse at the institute, who was a stern woman. Of course, not one of them would have stood up to the head nurse had she been there. When they were at work, they were all afraid of her. But when they were on their outings, they could let loose because their boss was nowhere around. Although Luisa actually liked and admired Frau Huber, she wanted the other girls to like and accept her, so she attempted to do an imitation of Huber. She wasn't very good. Still, the others laughed, and it made her feel warm and welcome in her new career.

CHAPTER 24

Luisa enjoyed earning a decent salary for the first time in her life. And now she finally had enough extra money to ask Paula to come for a visit. She knew Paula didn't have enough money for train fare, so she planned to pay for everything. Excited, she picked up the telephone receiver and instructed the operator to connect her to Paula.

"One moment, please," the operator said. There was a buzzing sound, then Paula picked up the phone.

"Hello."

"Paula, it's me, Luisa."

"Luisa! It's so good to hear your voice. It's been so long. How are you?"

"I'm doing well."

"How is your new job going?"

"I love it. And I'm sorry I haven't written. I've been so busy working. But I have good news. Because my job is going so well, I wanted to send you money to purchase a train ticket. I thought you might want to take a short holiday and come to visit me here. I'm out in the country and it is lovely. The air is fresh and . . . well, you could stay in my room with me."

"I would love that. I would love to see you again. But I

would have to get permission from my supervisor first. But I think that it should be all right because I've been reliable and have never taken a day off."

"Let me know when you get approval from your job, and when you're coming. As soon as I hear from you, I'll wire the money."

"I will. Oh, Luisa, I am so excited to be coming to see you," Paula said.

CHAPTER 25

Luisa went to her superior and requested permission for Paula to stay in her room with her for three nights. She told her superior that Paula was the younger sister of Adolf Hitler, and permission was instantly granted. Luisa, however, was still required to do her work during the day, but her evenings were free to spend with her friend. Then Luisa's superior looked Luisa in the eyes and said, "Now, you must not divulge anything about the euthanasia program at the institute to your friend. This is still top secret. Do you understand me?"

"Yes, of course. I would never tell anyone. Not even Paula. I swear it," she vowed.

Paula took the train and arrived at Luisa's dormitory early in the evening. When they saw each other, the two women hugged and laughed like schoolgirls.

"Oh, how I have missed you," Paula said. "I've missed your laugh and your stories."

"And I have missed you too. You've always been my most trusted friend."

"I have so much to tell you," Paula said.

"You arrived at a good time. I just finished my shift. Why

don't we go to a nice little café and have dinner and a few beers so we can catch up," Luisa suggested.

Paula smiled. She put her suitcase under Luisa's bed, and then the two girls walked toward town.

"You're right," Paula said. "It's lovely here. So peaceful. So far away from the hustle of the city."

"I know. It is such a serene place."

Luisa led Paula to a quiet little café, where they ordered dark beers and potatoes fried with onions.

"You look good," Paula said. "Your dress and your hair. It warms my heart to see you like this."

Luisa blushed. "Yes, I've finally taken your advice from so long ago. I bought myself some scented soap, and I set my hair every night. You look very good too. But then again you were always beautiful," Luisa answered, then she added, "So, tell me the news you have been holding back. I am about to burst with anticipation."

A big smile came over Paula's face. Then she took Luisa's hand in hers and said, "I've met someone, someone very special. His name is Erwin Jekelius. He's so very handsome that when I look at him, I swoon. Not only is he handsome but he is also a doctor. He's asked me to marry him."

"Did you accept?" Luisa's eyes grew wide.

"I did."

"Oh," Luisa gasped excitedly, "I want to know more. You must tell me all about him."

"As I said, he is so painfully handsome, and he treats me well." Paula smiled. "He's a psychiatrist and neurologist. He's very smart."

"Where does he work?"

"He works at the Steinhof psychiatric institution. I met him when I went there to see someone."

"You know someone in the institute?"

Paula leaned over and whispered into Luisa's ear, "Yes, I

am embarrassed to admit it, but my second cousin is institutionalized there. You won't tell anyone, will you?"

"Of course not. You're my best friend," Luisa confided in a whisper.

"I am so ashamed to have her as a part of our family. I can't stand the stares when I go into the hospital to see her. I went because Adolf asked me to go. He, too, is very agitated to have a family member who . . . well, you know, is not right. The truth is I am glad I went, because I met Erwin. But, just between us, I wish my cousin would just disappear. The shame of having someone like that in our family is horrible. To think, my second cousin, someone who shares my blood, is nothing but a useless eater."

"After we leave here, I have something to tell you on the way back to the dormitory. You must promise me that you will keep this a secret. My job depends on it," Luisa said.

"You know you can trust me."

They each had one more beer, and then Luisa insisted on paying the bill. "Are you sure?" Paula asked.

"I'm positive," Luisa said.

They left the restaurant and began walking back to the dormitory. Once they were outside and alone, Luisa looked to make sure no one else was around. Then she stopped walking and turned to look at Paula. She reached for Paula's hand and held it for a moment. Then taking a deep breath, she said, "I have something to share with you. But you must promise me that you will never tell anyone."

"I told you my secret. We've always known we could tell each other anything. Haven't we?"

Luisa nodded.

Then Paula squeezed her hand and said, "You have my promise that I will never tell anyone what you are about to tell me."

Luisa hesitated for a moment, then in a whisper, she said, "The work I am doing here at the Hadamar Institute is part of a very important project for the fatherland." Luisa cleared her throat. "It's top secret. If anyone ever finds out that I am telling you about it, I could lose my job. I might even be arrested."

Paula nodded.

"After all, someone must do these things. I mean, they are not pretty. But if we are to gain our rightful place . . ." Luisa began rambling.

"Do what, Luisa? You're talking in circles. I don't know what you are trying to tell me. Can you please start at the beginning?"

"The program that I am a part of is called T4."

"T4," Paula repeated. "I know about T4."

"How could you know? Like I said, it's top secret."

"My fiancé has also been an important part of the program."

"So, you know what it is?"

"Yes."

"You know everything? I mean everything?"

"You are speaking of the euthanasia."

Luisa nodded.

"Then, yes, I know," Paula said.

"I feel bad sometimes. I have to administer the final injection to several people each day," Luisa said.

"I understand how you feel. And this is a big responsibility. However, it is our duty to eliminate those who are unworthy of life. This is for the greater good. It is the only way our fatherland will grow and prosper," Paula said gently.

"I'm glad you understand."

"I do. Of course I do."

After Paula fell asleep, Luisa lay awake thinking. *I am happy for her that she's become engaged. She's found a man to take care of her. Paula will get married soon and be a hausfrau with babies at her heels.* Luisa smiled a sad smile. *But even though I am glad for her, I am jealous. I wish it would happen for me. Somehow, I don't think it will ever will. What girl doesn't want to be a wife and mother? That's our main purpose in life.* She glanced over at Paula who was sleeping soundly. *She's so much prettier than I am. She's my best friend, and I love her, but I have to admit, I'm envious. Soon she will embark on a new life, and I will still be single. I wish there was a doctor who was engaged to me. In truth, I wish any man at all wanted to marry me. I've never been asked. No one has ever shown any real interest in me.* She sighed out loud. *Well, at least I have an important career.*

CHAPTER 26

Paula's visit ended too soon. The two women hugged at the train station, promising to write. Paula waved from the window. Luisa managed a smile. Then she watched the train pull away and continued to keep her eyes on it until it was out of sight. Now, she would have to walk back to her dorm alone. Plopping down on a bench, she took a minute before heading back. Things had been all right before Paula had arrived. And now that Paula was gone, she was almost sorry she'd invited her to come visit. There was an emptiness in the pit of her stomach. *Paula is gone. Who knows if or when we will ever see each other again.*

To make things even worse, Paula's engagement to her doctor had changed things between them. In the past they had so much in common. They were two single women who were best friends. And even though they were far apart in distance, they had counted on each other for support through all the trials and tribulations of life. But now it seemed to Luisa that Paula had replaced her. She knew someone in her life whom she felt closer to than Luisa. And whenever Paula mentioned Erwin, Luisa felt left out. It was that same feeling she'd suffered from everyone but Paula in the past. And now, she felt it when she was with her best friend too.

It was not often Luisa arrived late to work. She took her job seriously and made an effort to always be on time. However, one evening a few weeks after Paula left, Luisa had been unable to fall asleep. After Paula's visit, she'd found herself to be depressed, and once again, as it had in the past, her hygiene began to suffer. She was unable to sleep or eat. It seemed to her that she had lost her friend forever. No one in her life had ever cared for her the way Paula had. And there was no end to the misery in sight.

This would not get better. In fact, it would probably get worse. *Soon Paula will have children and a home to take care of. She will have a husband whose needs will come first. In exchange, she will always feel wanted and loved. I am certain that once she is married, she will have no time to waste writing to me anymore. I wonder what it would be like to have someone waiting at home for me, someone who loved me and longed to hold me in his arms.* Then she thought of Noam, remembering how she had believed he loved her, and how foolish he'd made her feel when he left. Her entire body felt hot with rage. If he were standing right in front of her at that very moment, she was certain she would have torn him to pieces, like a wounded animal.

The hands of the clock moved, and the hours passed. *I must go to work in the morning. I need to sleep.* But she could not rest. Luisa finally drifted off when the sun began to rise. The alarm clock sounded. She jumped out of bed, disorientated. It had been a hard night. She'd only slept for two hours. Luisa put her uniform on as quickly as she could. Without washing her face or brushing her teeth, she ran all the way to her station. Even so, she was late to work by fifteen minutes. Her supervisor had been writing something on a chart when she looked up to see Luisa walk in. The supervisor shook her head, giving Luisa a look of disappointment.

"I'm sorry," Luisa said sincerely.

"Get to work. You should know better than to be late. Because you are late, other people cannot do their job properly. If this department is to run smoothly, everyone must arrive on time. Everyone is responsible to do their part, Luisa."

All day Luisa was worried that she would lose her job. But when she saw her supervisor late that afternoon, it seemed that she had forgotten about Luisa's tardiness.

The day went quickly because Luisa was extremely busy. The night nurse had not finished her work, leaving extra work behind for Luisa. This had been going on for several months, but Luisa never told anyone. She didn't want to lose this job. And so she chose not to call attention to herself by complaining. After she finished her shift that day, Luisa went to the office to pick up her pay envelope. Inside, she found a note. When she saw the note, she felt sick to her stomach. I hope this isn't a note telling me I've been terminated for being late. Her hands shook as she opened it and read.

Mandatory meeting in the meeting room on Thursday of next week at ten in the morning. Please arrive at least five minutes early.

Luisa hated meetings. They always made her nervous. She was always afraid that she would be asked a question which she had no answer for. *At least I am not being terminated.* She let out a sigh of relief. *And since the meeting is mandatory, I know I must attend. I'll use this as my opportunity to show my supervisor that I am not getting lazy or taking my job for granted. I'll shower and wash my hair. I'll look professional. And, most importantly, I'll be on time.*

Luisa was one of the first to arrive at the meeting room that Thursday morning. She found a seat in the back, where she hoped that if she sat quietly, she would not be asked any questions. Then she waited. By ten, everyone had arrived. They all looked fresh faced and ready to work.

"Heil Hitler!" Frau Huber saluted after she walked up to the front of the room.

"Heil Hitler!" The nurses all stood up and returned the salute.

"Well, well, all of you certainly do look splendid on this fine morning. Perfect examples of Aryan women working for our führer and our cause." Frau Huber smiled. Then she began. "I've called all of you here because we have an important matter to discuss this morning. Let me begin by saying that we are very pleased with your work. Each of you is doing a wonderful job of carrying out our mission. However, our superiors are finding that administering the injections one by one is just too slow a process. As you have noticed, we have a long waiting period from the time a patient arrives until we can deal with the problem. When we began T4, we had hoped that a patient would arrive and be handled the same day. However, it seems that there are just too many of them for that. Therefore, I am pleased to announce that we will be testing a new method of handling the problem. This week, special chambers will be installed in our facility. This new method is much more efficient. It will allow us to handle a hundred patients at the same time instead of individual injections." She stopped and took a breath. Then she looked around the room and smiled.

What a showman Frau Huber is. She is so confident. I wish I could be so self-assured, Luisa thought. *She is so good on a stage. If we were living in different times, I'll bet she would have been an actress.*

The facility I am speaking of will appear to be a shower room. You will tell your patient that they are going to be given a shower. It is your responsibility to keep your patients calm as you wheel them in. We must not have mass hysteria here, because a large group of people with mental problems could easily become dangerous. Speak to them in a soft and reassuring voice; explain that it will only be a quick shower, and after they are finished, you will give them some cookies and milk. Once the room is full, you must make sure you have gotten out. This is very important because what is about to take place in that room could cause your death. Once you have reported to the guard outside the door of the room, it will be sealed for your safety. And please remember that you may not enter the room again until you are told it is safe to do so.

Several of the nurses asked questions.

"What is going to happen in the room?"

"Are the patients going to be euthanized?"

Frau Huber avoided answering. She just nodded and said, "That's all for today. You will be receiving further instructions soon."

The special shower room was installed. Whenever Luisa passed it, she wondered exactly how it was going to work. Then once it began operating, Luisa and several other nurses who worked with her on her floor were invited to watch one of the first gassings. It went smoothly. The nurses did as they had been instructed. They each wheeled or walked their patients into the chamber. Then they told them they would return for them as soon as they had taken a shower and promised them treats once their shower was complete.

Luisa shuddered as she heard the metal door slam. It was a loud and terrifying sound. There was a small peephole. She looked inside. There was a hissing sound as the gas began to rise. Then there was coughing and choking. Luisa was unnerved the patients did not die easily. They screamed and clawed at each other seeking air to breathe. They urinated, defecated, and vomited. Luisa's stomach turned as she looked at the man who had administered the gas. "Are you sure that gas can't seep out here into this hall?"

"Positive. The room is sealed. You're perfectly safe here. I promise you," he said.

The patients' screams echoed through the room like a human slaughterhouse. And then there was an eerie silence.

Luisa had not even realized that Frau Huber was standing beside her. The older woman put her hand on Luisa's shoulder. Luisa jumped. "I saw a gassing. And I realize that it's a little overwhelming the first time. But I promise you that you will get used to it. It is so efficient, and it handles such a large number of patients at once, making our job so much easier. Now, we must wait a little while, and then we'll send in a couple of patients and have them clean up the room. Tell them that if they tell anyone what they saw here, they will be next in line."

"Yes, Frau Huber," Luisa said.

"And, by the way, Luisa . . ."

"Yes, ma'am?"

"Make sure that the patients who you choose to send in for the cleanup are in the next group to be processed. Give them sedatives to keep them quiet so they don't alarm the others."

"Yes, ma'am."

CHAPTER 27

Frau Huber was right. By the end of the week, Luisa had grown accustomed to the process. And considering that each day more patients were arriving, she felt it was an efficient way to deal with the problem. The hospital liked to have a patient euthanized within twenty-four hours of arrival, and the new gas chamber made that possible.

Then one morning as Luisa was helping to fill the gas chamber with patients, she happened to look up and see a woman with curly blonde hair being pushed in a wheelchair by a red-haired nurse. They were headed into the gas chamber. Luisa stopped walking and studied the patient for a moment. The skin around the woman's azure-blue eyes looked like dark, caved-in circles. Her golden locks were thin and greasy and fell about her head in unruly knots. Luisa walked over to the nurse who was wheeling the patient. "One moment, please, before you take her any farther. I think that I have special instructions for this patient."

The nurse stopped and waited. Luisa bent down and looked directly into the blonde patient's eyes. *Could it be her?* Luisa thought. *She is certainly older. But then, of course, she would be.*

And she looks like she's been through a great deal. Of course, being in a mental hospital could do that. But all in all, I think it's her.

"What is your name?" Luisa demanded of the patient who stared at her blankly. "Your name?"

"Goldie."

"Goldie Birnbaum?"

"Yes. I am Goldie Birnbaum. I need my medication. Please. I must have it. Can you get it for me?"

She doesn't recognize me. She doesn't know who I am, Luisa thought. A wicked smile came over Luisa's face. *What luck to have found Goldie here in this place where I have complete power over her.*

"I'll take the patient from here," Luisa told the nurse. "I was told to find this patient and bring her to the doctor's office."

"But she is scheduled for the special shower room," the red-haired nurse said, and she started wheeling Goldie inside the gas chamber.

"I understand. I'll take responsibility for her."

"Very well." The nurse walked away. "Do what you must with her. I'll go back to the rooms and get another one that's on the list for today."

Luisa smiled at the nurse.

"When are you getting me my medication?" Goldie asked.

"You don't remember me, do you?" Luisa asked.

"Should I?"

"We're old friends, Goldie Birnbaum. You humiliated me in school because I was too poor to buy clothes. Don't you remember? When you saw that your mother had given me your old clothes, you told everyone, and they all laughed at me. Remember me now?"

Goldie shrugged.

"Luisa Eisenreich. I am Luisa Eisenreich."

Goldie's eyes flew open at the mention of that name.

"Oh yes, you do remember now, don't you? We are old friends." Luisa gave her a wink and a wicked smile.

"I want the other nurse," Goldie said. "Please, I need to see the other nurse. Where is the other nurse? I am afraid of you."

"And well you should be. You should have thought of the future when you made me look like a fool. You certainly enjoyed it when everyone was laughing at me because you made me into a joke."

"I'm sorry. I was young. I didn't know what I was doing. Please, get the other nurse."

"And give up this lovely opportunity to visit with an old friend? Not a chance," Luisa said then let out a laugh. "I'll tell you what is about to happen to you. Would you like to know?"

"NO. I want the other nurse," Goldie said, her voice panicked.

"Well, I'll tell you anyway. The beautiful, rich Goldie Birnbaum, that's you"—Luisa pinched Goldie's cheek—"is about to be gassed to death. The gas that will steal your breath is about to come right out of those showerheads." Luisa pointed up the showerheads. "And there is nothing you can do to stop it. You will never have another chance to wear your fur coat or your pretty dresses. This is the end of the line for you: you'll never leave this place alive."

Goldie was shaking. She said, "Please, I'll do anything you want. I need to see the other nurse."

"She's gone. She left you in my care."

"Luisa, I am a sick woman. I just want to go home. I need my mother. Please, Luisa, take pity on me."

Luisa laughed, and then she turned to leave. But before she walked out of the room, she turned back and looked at Goldie. Then she smiled. She walked over and patted Goldie's arm. Then she wheeled her out of the room. "You're coming with me," she said.

"Thank you, Luisa. I always knew you were a good person at heart," Goldie said.

"Did you?" Luisa laughed. Then she took Goldie into a

storage closet with a cot and a chair. She quietly closed the door behind her and locked it. Then she looked at Goldie and said, "Now the time has come for you to pay back an old debt. Goldie Birnbaum, a quick death is too good for you."

"Please Luisa. My mother will give you money. She'll give you whatever you want. Just call her. Please. I don't feel well. I need my medication."

Luisa let out a short laugh, then she looked into Goldie's eyes and, running her tongue over her lower lip, she said, "This is going to be fun."

Luisa stared at Goldie for a few minutes. *How is it that you are still beautiful? Even drugged up and unkempt, you are still beautiful. I am going to make you pay for that beauty. I am going to make you pay for everything the Jews have made me endure throughout my life. You cruel, heartless, selfish bitch.*

CHAPTER 28

Luisa kept Goldie in that broom closet of a room for a little over a month. No one cared. She spent her time off torturing Goldie. The other doctors and nurses who discovered Goldie in that room, chose to ignore the situation. Luisa shaved Goldie's hair and saved a lock of it in her handbag. She gave Goldie just enough food to stay alive. She denied her the medication that helped her to cope. Each day, Luisa found unique ways to torture Goldie. And Luisa would have been happy to continue to brutalize this woman and punish her for every insult she'd ever suffered had she not received news from her superiors that the T4 program was about to be eliminated.

Luisa was miserable. She'd come to enjoy everything about this job, and now it was about to end. She was about to lose her excellent salary as well as the power this program gave her. More importantly, though, she wanted to make sure Goldie did not get out of the institution alive. So she knew she must act fast, because if Goldie were still alive once the program ended, she had a chance of survival. That afternoon, filled with regret, Luisa wheeled Goldie into the gas chamber.

"This is it for you," she said. "I'll miss our lovely afternoons together. But it's time for you to die."

Goldie cried and begged, "Please, Luisa. Please, let me go home. My parents will give you anything you want."

Luisa smiled. She shook her head. The beatings and cigarette burns she'd given Goldie had scarred Goldie's pretty face. Her golden locks were gone. Luisa kept her hair shaved to the scalp. Goldie had lost her lovely shape; starvation left her looking like a skeleton. *Now she is no longer beautiful,* Luisa thought.

"What a shame." Luisa clicked her tongue. "We could have been friends when we were back in school. But you thought you were too good for me. Don't you remember I told you that the day would come when the Jews would pay for everything they stole from the good German people? Well, that day has come."

"Luisa, I never stole anything."

"You stole my dignity. You made me feel like I was dirt under your feet. And now it's time to pay the price. Sorry, Goldie Birnbaum, but you are all finished. Soon you will die a painful death, and I'll be watching right through that window." Luisa pointed to the small window in the chamber.

Then she left.

That night Luisa lay in her bed thinking about Goldie. *I should feel satisfaction. I was victorious. And yet, all I feel is empty. It is over now. At least while she was still alive, I felt that she was paying for what she did. But now, she is dead. I will have no more opportunity to make her suffer the way she made me suffer. To make matters worse, the T4 program is closing, and I don't know what I am going to do from here. I no longer feel that I can be an ordinary nurse. The power I felt in this program set me on fire. It gave me purpose. I was no longer the stone everyone kicked around. I was in control. I had the power to end a life.*

Luisa knew the procedure that took place when a patient was euthanized. The family would receive a telegram telling them that their loved one had passed away either from a heart attack or a disease. The telegram would be sent over to the Birnbaums in the next week or so. And since Luisa hated

Esther Birnbaum, she decided the woman deserved to know the truth about how her precious, spoiled daughter died. *Since the program is ending in a few days anyway, and there is no need for secrets anymore, I'll take pleasure in returning to Berlin to make sure Frau Birnbaum knows everything that happened down to the last horrific detail.*

The following morning, Luisa packed her things. Then she waited a few days until she received the notice that informed her that the program was canceled and she was no longer needed at the institute. While the other nurses were in tears hugging each other and saying their goodbyes, Luisa was already on her way to the train station. She wanted to be at Frau Birnbaum's house on the day the telegram arrived.

After she returned to Berlin, Luisa went back to rent the room she'd left in the woman's hotel. Then each day before the sun rose, she waited outside the Birnbaum home. She was afraid she'd missed the telegram, because it took four days to arrive. But then she saw a messenger boy on a bicycle ride up to the door. *That's it.* She smiled. *That's the telegram. Esther is about to face her worst nightmare.* She watched the boy ride away. Then she walked up to the door and knocked. Hans Hubermann, the Birnbaums' driver, answered the door.

"Yes, can I help you?" he asked.

"I'm here to see Frau Birnbaum," Luisa said, trying to control the shock she felt at seeing him. She remembered Hans Hubermann. She'd seen him driving Goldie to school. He was older now, more weathered, but it was him. Luisa knew that Hans was not a Jew. He was an Aryan. It was illegal for him to still be working for the Birnbaums. Yet here he was. *How dare he?*

"Won't you please come inside? I'll let Frau Birnbaum know you're here. May I have your name?"

"Tell her Luisa Eisenreich has come to give her some very important information."

Hans nodded. Then he walked away, leaving her to wait, and went into another room. It was a couple of minutes before he returned. "I'm sorry. Frau Birnbaum has received some bad news today, and she is unable to receive guests. Perhaps you can return in a week or so?"

"I must see her now," Luisa said, pushing past Hans and entering the room he'd just come out of.

"Hello, Frau Birnbaum. Do you remember me?" Luisa asked. "Luisa Eisenreich?"

It was clear to Luisa that Esther was distressed. "Yes, of course I remember you. But I'm sorry, Luisa, I can't speak with you today. I've just learned that my daughter passed away."

"Such a shame. I knew Goldie. I'm sure you remember that too. What did she die from?"

"A heart attack. She was in a hospital."

Luisa picked up the telegram and read it. Then she shook her head, and a sly smile appeared on her face. "I have something to tell you," she said in a singsong voice. "Pretty little Goldie didn't die from a heart attack. She was murdered."

"Murdered? What are you talking about, Luisa?"

Luisa reached into her handbag and grabbed a bunch of golden, curly hair; she threw the curls on the desk in front of Esther. "Does this hair look familiar to you?"

Esther's eyes filled with horror.

"I was Goldie's nurse. Oh yes, Frau Birnbaum, I am a nurse now. I'm not the poor, wretched girl you knew. I am an Aryan nurse."

Esther stared at the hair on the desk. "It's Goldie's hair," she said softly, almost choking on the words.

"Yes, that's right. It is Goldie's hair. I shaved her head before she died. I wanted to make sure she was destroyed and broken even before she died. So that meant she would have to see herself without her lovely hair. But I thought you deserved to have it. In case you haven't realized it yet, Frau Birnbaum, I killed Goldie. It was me. She deserved it. She was a good-for-nothing, rotten Jew rat just like you. I threw your precious daughter into a gas chamber, then I watched her suffer as the life was sucked out of her. By the way, perhaps you would like to know how the gas works? I can tell you."

"Get out of my home," Esther Birnbaum growled, her voice deep, angry, and firm.

"Oh, and how she suffered. You should have seen it. She was crying for you. Mother, I want my mother. It was pitiful."

"Hans," Esther called out. "Hans, please, come here."

He came right away. "Yes, Frau Birnbaum?"

"Take this woman out of my home."

Hans went to grab Luisa, but she shook him off and headed for the door. "No need. I'm leaving."

Luisa left the house. She thought torturing Frau Birnbaum would bring her the satisfaction she needed, but she still felt empty inside.

As she walked toward the hotel where she was living, she thought, *I know I am superior to those Jews. I've killed plenty of them. So why do I still feel like the worthless, poor child I was when I was growing up?* She shook her head and continued walking. *I am so angry at Hans. How can a pure Aryan man break the law and work for Jews? And what about the fact that the Birnbaums' home should already have been confiscated and given to deserving Germans? Yet, somehow, they are still living there, and Hans is still working for them. What kind of magic Jew spell has that bitch cast to keep that house? Well, I am not done with her. Now, not only must I make Esther pay, but Hans, because he's betrayed his own people and should pay an even greater price.*

When Luisa got back to her apartment, she sat down at her little desk and wrote to Paula.

Dear Paula,

The T4 program at Hadamar has been canceled, and now I am out of work again. I have been thinking about applying for a job working with the Deutscher Mädels. I've worked with them in the past and I enjoyed it. I like teaching the young women about our fatherland and what is expected of them. They look up to me, and it makes me feel good. I know that I worked hard to become a nurse. I wanted it so badly, but after the T4 program, I find that I have changed. So, I think perhaps I'll take a short break from nursing. I will probably return to it later on down the road. But for now, I think I will do something else.

Anyway, I had an experience today that left me feeling angry. And since I have no one here that I feel close enough to talk to, I thought I would write to you about it. I don't know how you feel about this, but in my humble opinion there is nothing more despicable than an Aryan who would defy our führer and work for a Jew. Today I encountered such a man. It has been on my mind all day, and I've considered turning him in to the authorities, but I think I'll wait and see if he makes an even greater mistake. The Jews have a big house and lots of money that should already have been confiscated. They must have some kind of connections. But it's just a matter of time before someone finds out and the home is confiscated. Then they'll be taken away, unless of course, that Aryan man should go so far as to hide the Jews he works for. I believe he just might. And that would cost him even more dearly. So my plan is this: I'll follow him home each night. If I am working with the Deutscher Mädels, I'll be able to do that. And I'll keep watch on his house and see what I can find out. I'll let you know.

Enough about me. I just needed to tell someone about what I saw. So, how are things going with you and Erwin? Have you set a date for the wedding? When I was earning a nice salary with the T4 program, I would have tried to come to Austria for the wedding, but now I don't know if I'll have enough money. The Deutscher Mädels pay well, but it doesn't pay as well as the program did. So I'll have to wait and see.

Your friend, Luisa.

CHAPTER 29

Luisa enjoyed her job as leader of the Deutscher Mädels. It wasn't as important as being a nurse, and she didn't have the power to murder that she had at Hadamar. But she did have some degree of power and respect. And for now, it was better than working at a regular hospital. She was the leader of a group of young girls who were required to obey her. Luisa was much older than the other leaders. And the girls thought she was wise. They were constantly trying to impress her, and they listened to everything she told them. It was hard not to like this job.

Each night she waited outside the Birnbaums' house and followed Hans home, and between her Deutscher Mädels meetings, she kept a watch on his house. Luisa wanted to see how far he would go in his willingness to break the law. She wasn't surprised one afternoon when she went to the Birnbaum house. It was locked up, and the Birnbaums were gone. The house was dark. She went by the following day, and there as still no one there. *They're gone and Hans is gone too. They must have run away in the middle of the night. I hope they haven't escaped the country somehow. I hope he is hiding them.*

She took the bus to Hans's home and saw the Birnbaums'

automobile parked out front. *He has their car. This is rich. Either they have left the country or he's hiding them,* Luisa thought. *And I am going to find out more. I am going to find out the whole story, and then I am going to expose them. I want to be sure they are in his house before I alert the authorities.*

CHAPTER 30

Dear Luisa,

I couldn't be more in agreement with you. No Aryan person should befriend Jews. Never, not under any circumstances. Not only is it dangerous, but it is also against the law. If I were you, I would see to it that this man pays for his crime.

As far as Erwin and I are concerned, we haven't set a date yet. We are eagerly awaiting permission to marry. As soon as we receive it, I'll let you know.

Your friend, Paula.

Dear Paula,

It is done. The Jews have been caught. I was right! I knew I was right all along! The Aryan driver and his wife were hiding them in the attic of their home. They have been arrested. The best part of their arrest was seeing their faces, because they were betrayed by their own son. I am proud to say that I can take credit for this arrest because I did have a hand in it. I set everything up so that their son would turn them in. It's a long story, but I met him at a meeting when my group of girls from the Deutscher Mädels had a camping trip with a group of Hitler Youth. He was one of the Hitler Youth. How strange that his name is Erwin, just like your fiancé's name.

He did something he shouldn't have done and that brought him to my attention. Well, can you imagine how I felt when I saw his surname and I realized who he was? It was quite easy to manipulate him into turning his parents in. And since I knew that a betrayal from his own son would be more devastating to the Aryan driver than being turned in by me, a stranger, I arranged it. Everything went as planned, and I know I should feel gratified, but I don't. Don't get me wrong, I am glad they will all pay for their crimes against our beloved fatherland. However, I am growing bored working with the Deutscher Mädels. I know it's important to teach our youth. However, cooking, cleaning, and sports have become my life, and I just don't feel stimulated by my job. I wish I could find something more fulfilling. Something more like the T4 program.

Your friend, Luisa.

CHAPTER 31

Several months passed without any correspondence from Paula. Luisa missed her. But when she tried to telephone, the operator said Paula had moved. Luisa hung the receiver back in its cradle and sat down dazed, confused, and frightened. *I wouldn't think that she would have run off and gotten married without sending me a forwarding address. We have been best friends for so many years that I am sure if she could, she would have let me know where she was going. I am worried about her. What if something bad happened to her? I will never know. Because no one would ever think to contact me.*

Luisa was shattered. Paula had been her only true friend, and now she was unable to get in contact with her. She hoped with all her heart that Paula was all right. And each day she checked the mail, her heart pounding, for a letter that didn't arrive.

Winter came, blanketing Germany in snow. Ice crystals hung from the trees. In the past Luisa had marveled at the icicles. She knew they were dangerous and could hurt you if they fell on you. But even so, they were so magnificent that, when she was a child, she would often daydream that the fatherland was an icy kingdom of beautiful Nordic warriors.

But not this winter. Luisa was sad and lonely this winter.

Her body felt chilled from the inside out. Her heart was broken by the loss of her friend, and she felt her loneliness even more intensely than usual. Working with teenage girls each day, with their constant exuberance, youth, and enthusiasm was starting to get on her nerves. Sometimes she wanted to quit, but she couldn't; she needed the money. So she dragged herself to meetings and repeated the same old rhetoric. And then one afternoon when she returned from work, she found a letter waiting for her. She immediately recognized the swirly handwriting. Her heart thumped in her chest as she tore open the envelope.

Dear Luisa,

I wanted to write to you sooner, but I couldn't because I was very depressed. I am so sorry, but I didn't get out of bed for several months. But now that I am finally able to get back to living, I have so much to tell you. The reason my heart was broken, and I went into such a bleak depression, was because my wedding is off. My brother, Adolf, forbade me to marry Erwin. He said that he, and he alone, would decide who could be a member of our family. He said that Erwin was not worthy, and he was angry that I even asked for his blessing. First, I begged him to reconsider. When he refused, I fought him on it. Nothing would change his mind. He told me that not only did I require his blessing to marry, but because of who he is, I require his permission. Sometimes I can't stand him. He can be so hard and difficult.

Then, to make matters worse, in order to punish Erwin and maybe me too, Adolf sent Erwin to the Eastern Front to serve as a soldier. My dear fiancé was not a warrior. He was an educated man, a doctor, and he couldn't fight. So, he was killed in action. I broke down even further when I learned of Erwin's death. I couldn't eat or sleep. I was afraid I was going to need to be institutionalized. But, of course, I knew the dangers of that firsthand. Both you and Erwin had shared the truth with me of what happens to those people. I was afraid, so I forced myself to get out of bed and try to get on with life. I was still very depressed.

Then I received a letter with a job offer to work as a secretary in a military field hospital on the Eastern Front. I can't say whether Adolf had anything to do with the offer or not. But as soon as I got the offer, I thought of Erwin. I thought of how difficult it must have been for him when he was alone and out there in the East, fighting. My darling Erwin is gone now. I have to face that. But then I thought, how many others like him are out there on the front, all alone, desperately in need of a friend, of someone German to comfort them? It was then I knew that it was my duty and my destiny to serve the soldiers. So, I am now living in the East. I was wondering how you would feel about joining me here. We are always in need of nurses. I can get you a job. And being here, I can see how badly our German soldiers need us German women to help them. Let me know what you decide.

Your friend, Paula.

Luisa was so happy to hear from Paula that tears spilled down her cheeks. *A military field hospital. I don't know if I would like that at all. Still, if I take the job, I'll be working with Paula. And that would be wonderful to be so close to her. We could have our weekly card games and dinners again. It's been such a long time since we lived in the same area. I might even meet a soldier and fall in love. If that's even possible anymore for a woman like me.* She let out a short laugh. *I'm in my late forties, certainly not young. It's sad, but almost funny, but to be loved was the thing I wanted most out of life when I was a girl. And it is the only thing I can say that I have never experienced. I've felt love, but it has never been returned. Perhaps I am too jaded now to ever let myself care that much for anyone again. But at least if I go to work at this field hospital, then I would have my friend to talk to. And I am bored with the Deutscher Mädels. This could be just the change I need.*

Luisa decided that she would take the job and wrote a quick note to Paula telling her as much. It wasn't until she began to fill out the envelope that she realized the letter had not come from Paula's old address. Luisa said the word aloud: "The Eastern Front. That's in the direction of Russia." She was a little frightened at the thought of traveling into the East, but she was also a little excited.

CHAPTER 32

Luisa was thrilled to see Paula again, even if the military hospital didn't offer as many comforts as she would have liked. It was a makeshift hospital, a tent rather than a building, that had been set up to care for wounded soldiers only ten miles from the battlefront. The work was grueling. Not only was she required to assist the doctors in emergency surgeries, dress wounds, and administer medicines, but the soldiers depended on Luisa to comfort them as they struggled in terrific pain. Many of them died in her arms. She tried to show them compassion. But she felt none. All she felt was the loss of power.

This nursing job was nothing like her job at Hadamar. There were no outings with her coworkers. She had no power over the patients. They were pathetic young men moaning in pain, constantly needing something from her. Her hours were not definite. She was expected to work whenever she was needed, and that was often with very little time for rest. Luisa was angry. She'd traveled East to this horrible place to enjoy some time with her friend. But there was no time to spare. Depression set in, and she began to take time off, claiming she was too ill to work.

Her supervisor, Frau Graf, an older woman who had been a nurse for many years, and who had seen combat in the Great War as well has this one, had seen this happen with other nurses and soldiers as well. She had a solution. One evening as Luisa was headed back to her makeshift room, which was really nothing more than a curtained-off area with a foldable cot, her supervisor stopped her.

"Luisa," Frau Graf called out.

Luisa turned to see her supervisor headed toward her. She wanted to scream. *Please don't tell me I must work another shift. I'm exhausted. I hate this place. I want to go to bed.* "Yes," Luisa said.

"I have something for you. It will help you feel better."

"I feel fine," Luisa lied.

"I know how hard this job is, Luisa. I've been working in field hospitals most of my life. I am going to give you a very special chocolate bar. Eat one quarter of it tomorrow before you start your shift. It will give you energy and help you to feel much better about your work."

Luisa took the chocolate bar. She loved chocolate. Eyeing the bar greedily, she nodded and smiled.

Seeming to read her mind, Frau Graf said, "Don't eat it tonight. This is not regular chocolate. It's something special. If you eat it tonight, you won't be able to sleep. Get a good night's rest, and then eat it after breakfast tomorrow."

"Thank you, Frau Graf," Luisa said, tucking the candy bar into the pocket of her uniform.

"And Luisa, don't eat the entire bar. That could be very dangerous. Eat only one quarter each day. Do you understand me?"

"Yes, and thank you."

Luisa did as Frau Graf instructed and ate a quarter of the chocolate bar after she finished breakfast the following day. She felt a surge of energy and well-being bubble up through her entire body. No longer did she dread her work, but she embraced it. In fact, she couldn't wait to be busy. The more work she had to do that day, the better she liked it. Later that afternoon, she ran into Paula and told her about the candy.

"I know about that chocolate," Paula said. "It's called *panzerschokolade*. It contains methamphetamine. It's the methamphetamine that is giving you all of this energy."

"It's a wonder drug," Luisa said. "I love it. I feel so good."

"Yes, it is an amazing drug. I have taken it, too, whenever I have been able to get it."

That evening after Luisa finished her shift, she went to visit with Paula. They stayed up late. Finally, Luisa went back to her own small area, but she was unable to sleep. She lay on her cot, waves of energy pulsing through her veins. *I could take on another shift right now.* She got out of bed and went to search for Frau Graf. She wanted to ask Frau Graf if she would like her to work another shift.

"I'm sorry, but Frau Graf won't be here at the hospital for work until seven this morning."

"Thank you," Luisa said. She went back to her cot and did some of the exercises she remembered from the drills with the Deutscher Mädels. She did push-ups and sit-ups and lunges. But nothing exhausted her. She was wide awake.

At exactly seven o'clock, Luisa went back to the hospital ward to speak with Frau Graf.

"Heil Hitler!" Luisa said when she saw Frau Graf.

"Heil Hitler! Don't you look perky this morning," she said, smiling.

"The chocolate was very effective. I could easily have worked a double shift yesterday. And I felt so alive and good."

"Yes, I know. The soldiers use it to avoid exhaustion on the battlefield. However, you are going to find that you will be very tired at about four this afternoon. When the exhaustion comes over you, just break off a corner of the bar and eat it. It will help you finish your shift. Then just start again with a quarter of the bar tomorrow morning."

"I will."

"And when this chocolate bar runs out, just come and see me. I'll give you another one."

"Thank you, Frau Graf."

CHAPTER 33

By the time two months passed, Luisa found she needed a half of the bar instead of a quarter each morning to get that same burst of energy. She hardly slept, and instead of the original feelings of well-being that she had when she ate the chocolate, now she found that she was angry all the time. One afternoon she lost patience with a young soldier who was dying. She yelled at him for speaking too slowly and begging her to sit with him.

"You are not my only patient," she said. "I have others. I can't sit here and waste my entire morning with you."

Frau Graf gently reprimanded Luisa and reminded her that the soldiers were giving their lives for the fatherland. "We must be kind to them," she said. "We are their nurses. We are the only connection they have to their German roots."

When the Pervitin wore off, Luisa fell asleep no matter where she was. And she began to have terrible nightmares from which she awakened shaking and unnerved. Most of her dreams were the same. In her dreams the patients from the T4 program came alive and began chasing her. She would awaken with her pulse pounding and her head aching. Still, she continued to take the Pervitin, and as the months progressed, she began to hallucinate while she was awake. Luisa began confusing the medications she gave to the patients. And because of this, the doctors found her to be responsible for more than one death. She was reprimanded for her negligence, but still, they did not fire her.

Then, one afternoon, an extremely large group of severely wounded men were delivered to the hospital. They needed immediate attention. The work was strenuous. There was no time to take a break. Luisa was feeling overwhelmed. She had eaten an entire bar over the course of that morning. That was because no matter how much of the Pervitin she took, she was still not feeling strong enough to handle the workload. She was sweating profusely, and she was dizzy.

"I need to go and lie down," Luisa told her superior. "I feel sick, like I might vomit."

"I'm sorry. You can't leave. We have a disaster here. We need you."

"But I don't feel well."

"You have a job to do. I don't like to see weakness in our nurses. It is just not tolerated. Now stop wasting my time and get back to work."

Luisa put her hand into the pocket of her uniform where she had another chocolate bar. Breaking off a piece, she stuffed it into her mouth. She'd never taken this much Pervitin at once. The room was spinning. She sunk down into a chair. All around her the doctors and nurses were racing from patient to patient. Luisa couldn't move. But then she felt a rush of blood go to her head. Her body trembled, followed by that strong surge of energy that she had come to depend upon. *I can do this. I feel better, stronger all ready.*

Luisa straightened her back and walked over to the next patient in line to be treated. But when she looked into the face of the patient on the cot, she didn't see the young man who was lying there, who had suffered a wound to his face. Instead, she hallucinated and saw Goldie Birnbaum with half of her face blown off. The sweat began pouring down from her armpits and dripping from her forehead.

"What are you doing here?" Luisa asked, frightened and angry. "You're dead. I killed you."

"I'm not dead," the soldier said. "Help me, please. I need your help. I am in terrible pain."

"I would never help you, Jew. How did you live through that gas? No one could live through that."

"I don't know what you're talking about. I need something for the pain." It was the soldier speaking. But in Luisa's mind it was Goldie.

"I am glad you are in pain. You deserve to be in pain."

"Help me. Someone help me," the soldier began calling out. "This nurse is crazy."

One of the doctors heard the soldier as he was walking by. "What is going on here?"

"This woman is a Jew. I don't know what she is doing here in this hospital, she should be dead. I killed her. But I promise you, Doctor, I am certain that she is a Jew. And I am going to be forced to kill her again," Luisa said. Then she took a pillow and began to smother the soldier. The doctor threw Luisa off the patient and grabbed the pillow.

"What the hell are you doing?" He stared at Luisa, his eyes wide with shock.

"I am telling you something. I know this Jew. I went to school with her."

It took two strong men to remove Luisa from the soldier's bedside. And that night she was fired. As she packed her things to leave the hospital, Paula entered her little makeshift room. "I heard what happened."

"I swear to you, it was Goldie in that bed."

"You were hallucinating," Paula said. She patted Luisa's hand.

"I know it was Goldie. I saw her. I am telling you, I saw her. They don't believe me. They are sending me away. I am going back home to Berlin. They don't want me here anymore. OH, Paula, I will miss you."

"I will miss you too," Paula said, and she hugged Luisa. "But perhaps it was a mistake for you to come here. Perhaps you will be better off in Berlin." She breathed a sigh of relief.

CHAPTER 34

Luisa had mixed feelings about leaving her job. She was sad to be leaving Paula and returning to Berlin, although since her arrival, she'd hardly had enough time to herself to enjoy Paula's company. And she wasn't sorry to be leaving the front lines of battle. The job took all of her energy and was too demanding.

Luisa took the train back to Berlin, and then she moved back into the cheap room at the ladies' hotel where she'd spent most of her life.

Her service in the military hospital had changed her in many ways, the most pressing of which was that she returned from the Eastern Front with an addiction to Pervitin. This was an addiction that she could not ignore. If she couldn't get her hands on the drug, she was unable to function.

Luisa wrote to Paula and told her that she needed her help to acquire the drug. Paula complied by sending Luisa a small black box with tiny tablets inside and a note that read, "This is Pervitin. It is not in chocolate, but it's the same thing. Don't take more than two of these tablets at a time. It could be dangerous if you do."

Luisa needed a job. She went back to the Deutscher

Mädels, but they were not hiring. Then she applied for nursing positions at several local hospitals where she was rejected due to her poor references from the military. With few options left, she found a job as a cook at a small German restaurant. She was glad to be away from the battlefield. But she missed Paula. Each month she received a letter and another small box of pills, which she sent Paula money for. Luisa found she needed to take the pills two at time, but after a short time they were no longer supplying the energy rush she'd come to rely on. It wasn't that she needed the energy for her job anymore. She didn't. Her work was easy in comparison to the job she'd had in the military. But she was addicted to the feeling that she got from the Pervitin, so she began breaking off a tiny piece of a third pill and taking it.

CHAPTER 35

No one wanted to admit the truth, and everyone Luisa met in Berlin tried to pretend, but it was becoming obvious that Germany was losing the war. Russia was too powerful an enemy to defeat. Her soldiers were ruthless, and her winters were brutal.

Luisa was growing worried about what would happen to the German people once the German Army began to retreat.

Then one of the customers at the restaurant where Luisa worked came in with some very frightening news. He was a regular, a businessman who gathered with a group of his friends at the restaurant each morning before work. They talked about everything. And while Luisa cooked behind the counter, she listened. That morning, the man said that he'd read in the paper that Adolf Hitler had disappeared into his bunker along with Eva Braun and a few other high-ranking Nazi officers.

Luisa listened as the customers discussed the events.

"He's just planning another strategy," one of the businessmen said. "He'll come out and defeat those communists; you just wait and see."

"Yes, you're probably right," another agreed as he ate his eggs.

"I don't know about this. We have lost so many soldiers. All we have left to defend us here at home are young boys," a woman, who happened to overhear the conversation, said.

"I'm sure our führer has a plan. He will be victorious. You'll see. We are a race of victors. We will not lose this war," one man went on.

"I hope you're right," another answered.

Luisa listened. But she knew from Paula's letters that the Germans were already retreating from the Eastern Front. Russia was a powerful country. Even Dr. Goebbels admitted that the Russians were like bears, hardly human. Not only were the people fierce, but the winters were unbearable, much colder than German winters. And the troops did not have warm enough clothes to endure the weather. In her letters to Luisa, Paula had admitted the battles were not going well, but she always remained certain that somehow Germany would recover and be victorious. Luisa hoped Paula was right, but she was beginning to have doubts.

CHAPTER 36

Buried fifty-five feet beneath the chancellery, in an air raid shelter, Adolf Hitler and Joseph Goebbels discussed Fredrick the Great. They were hoping that somehow the Allies would fall. Stubbornly, Hitler refused to admit that he'd made any mistakes. "It will be all right. We will not lose this war," he said, but he still did not move to leave the bunker.

During the next 105 days, the führer entertained Himmler and Goring. He even left the bunker for a few hours once to decorate a group of Hitler Youth.

But Hitler knew the truth. Germany was losing the war. And he was losing power.

When it was absolutely certain that a German victory would be impossible, while still hiding down in the bunker, the führer married his girlfriend, Eva Braun. They planned to die together. Next, Dr. Josef Goebbels and his wife murdered their six young children and then killed themselves. Once the führer made certain his new bride was dead, it was said Hitler committed suicide. However, some believe the führer escaped to South America.

CHAPTER 37

When the news of Hitler's death reached Luisa, she let out a loud cry of despair that brought the landlady running to her door. The newspaper that Luisa had been reading dropped from her trembling hands. *I've spent my life serving this man and this government. Now we Germans are being left to fend for ourselves as the Russians come marching through our land to take the spoils.*

"Fräulein Eisenreich, are you all right in there?" the land-lady asked as she pounded her fist on the door.

"Yes, yes. I'm sorry. I'm fine," Luisa managed to say as she sank down onto the bed. She was battling so many emotions, most of all anger. *How could our führer do this to us?* The stimu-lants in her body made her sweat and tremble. She couldn't find a comfortable position. Luisa tossed and turned on the bed. Then she got up and sat in the chair. Still ill at ease, she lay her head on the desk and wept. It was almost nightfall. She had brought home some food from the restaurant, but even though she'd worked ten hours that day and had not eaten since morning, she had no appetite. Her stomach was in knots. *What is going to become of me?*

Picking up the paper again, she began to read where she'd left off. German women all along the Eastern Front were committing suicide rather than face the Russian Army. The word rape was mentioned several times, but Luisa could not read the sentences. She could not concentrate. The words blurred on the paper, and her eyes would not focus. Yet even though she could not read it, she knew what the article said. Russian soldiers were raping German women. They were punishing Germany's women for the brothers, sons, and fathers they'd lost in battle. And for the women they'd been forced to leave behind. Luisa was terrified. The thought of being raped by a Russian soldier who was as strong and fierce as a bear unnerved her.

She picked up a pen and began to write to Paula.

Dear Paula,

I read the newspapers. I am thoroughly disgusted with your brother. How could he abandon us and leave us to the mercy of the Russians? He was certainly not the hero we good Germans thought he was. No true Teutonic hero would leave his subjects, who supported him the way we have, to the mercy of the enemy. I have lost all respect for your brother. It seems he is little more than a coward. You should be ashamed.

I have included some money for my pills. I would appreciate your sending them as soon as possible.

Luisa.

Luisa was angry. She mailed the letter without taking the time to think of what the consequences would be.

A week later Luisa received a letter from Paula. This time the letter did not contain any pills.

Luisa,

You have always been an arrogant person. But because I thought you were my friend, I tolerated it. I put up with all your nonsense through the years and I never criticized you.

I allowed you to stay at my flat even though your hygiene was questionable at best. I stood by you when you almost cost me my job at the field hospital because of your insane behavior. Now, here I am suffering not only the loss of my fiancé, but the death of my brother as well, and instead of sympathy at the loss of my brother, you write this scathing and cruel letter to me. I have always stood by you no matter what happened. But I know now that you are not the person I thought you were. Perhaps you are nothing more than a vicious and horrible monster. I never want to see you or hear from you again. There will be no more medication coming to you from me. You will find the money you sent me for your pills in this envelope. You must find another way to acquire your Pervitin. I am done with you. I know you are hurt. I am hurt too. We all are. But your lashing out at me was more than I will tolerate. Remember, after all, no matter what he did wrong, he was still my brother.

Paula.

Luisa was stunned. She had lashed out without thinking. Since she'd started taking the Pervitin, she had been having emotional outbursts. *I should never have mailed that damn letter*, she thought.

Luisa checked her pillbox. There were only four pills left. Two days' worth, and that was if she took two a day. Recently she'd found that she needed an extra quarter of a pill just to have enough energy to complete her shift at work. She reread Paula's letter and found that she was sorry she'd written such harsh words to Paula. *It wasn't Paula's fault. It was Adolf's.* Still, she had never been one to say she was sorry, and even though she wanted to apologize, she tried but found she could not write an apology. Damn it, I need these pills. I must do something. Besides, I am going to miss Paula if I don't make amends somehow. Luisa sat down at her desk, took her pen in her hand, and wrote:

Dear Paula,
    I am sorry . . .

She crinkled up the paper and threw it in the trash. Then she let the pen fall onto the desk and began to weep. All night long she lay in bed shaking. She was shaking so hard that her teeth were chattering. In the morning she found that she'd broken one of her teeth. Luisa got out of bed, her hair still wet with sweat, and took the two pills. Then she dressed for work. But two pills weren't enough to energize her, so she took another half. Still, she felt depressed and groggy. By noon that day she took the other half leaving her only one pill for the next day. Fear gripped her as she realized she would be spiraling downward as soon as the effects wore off and she had no more pills to help her.

"Luisa, hurry up, you're staring out into space. I need that sauerbraten," the owner of the restaurant said as Luisa stood behind the counter.

Luisa nodded. But the sweat was running into her eyes. She couldn't control the shaking of her hands.

"Luisa? What's wrong with you?" The owner returned a few minutes later.

"Stop asking me. Shut up and stop asking me. I am going as fast as I can," she screamed. The patrons in the restaurant looked up from their newspapers and conversations to stare at the cook who was yelling. Luisa saw their astonished faces. She stared at them blankly. But then slowly each one of their faces began to change. They morphed into the faces of the patients who she'd euthanized at the Hadamar center. *Am I hallucinating or is this real? They look so real. But it's impossible. Isn't it? They're dead. They are all dead. Aren't they?*

"Luisa!" The owner slammed his fist on the counter.

"Leave me alone. Leave me alone," Luisa said, throwing her apron on the floor and running out the door of the restaurant. It was early May; the sky was cornflower blue. The sun was bright and golden. But Luisa could not see any of God's beautiful miracles. Instead, she saw the dead who she'd murdered, coming toward her. They were walking slowly toward her. She ran. They chased her and she kept running. Then she heard Esther's voice. She turned around. No one was there. She ran again, but Esther was calling her, "Luisa, Luisa." She stopped on the corner and turned around. Esther Birnbaum stood in front of her holding the lock of Goldie's hair that she'd thrown at her. "You are not real," Luisa said. "You are a hallucination."

Esther shook her head. "You are a sick girl, Luisa. You have hurt me and my family deeply. But, I forgive you."

"Don't forgive me, Esther Birnbaum. I did what I did because I knew it was right."

"You knew it wasn't. I would have helped you if you would have allowed me to. Instead, you murdered my only child. My Goldie. I know she wasn't perfect. No one is. Yet you had no forgiveness in your heart for her. I pity you."

"I don't want your pity."

Luisa was screaming in the street. A crowd was gathering around her. In that crowd, Luisa was certain she saw Goldie Birnbaum, young and beautiful again, and laughing at her.

Goldie walked up to her and said, "Look at you, Luisa Eisenreich. You're still nothing but a trashy pig. You may think you killed me, but you can't kill me. I will always be with you to remind you of everything you could never be."

Luisa lost her vision. She couldn't see anything but darkness. She had to get away, away from Goldie and Esther, so she began to run again.

There was a loud blare of horns honking. Luisa jumped. Tires screeched. Pain shot through Luisa as she fell to the pavement.

"Someone get help," a stranger said.

Luisa heard the strangers in the street, but she couldn't see them.

"I think she's dead."

"She's dying for sure."

I'm dying, Luisa thought. Then she saw Esther's face in her mind's eye. "I'm so afraid," Luisa said pathetically. I, who have administered death to so many people, find I am terrified now that I am facing it myself."

"It's all right. Close your eyes," Esther said. "You will be all right."

"Can you really forgive me?"

"I forgive you, Luisa. Because hating you, and carrying anger toward you, only hurts me more. You should have learned that. You carried so much hate in your heart for so long. I hope you realize that it never served you. In fact, that hate is what broke you and stole any chance you had to be happy. Now your time on earth is over. Ask for God's forgiveness, Luisa. Ask, and be truthful in your words. He is a merciful God."

AUTHORS NOTE

I always enjoy hearing from my readers, and your thoughts about my work are very important to me. If you enjoyed my novel, please consider telling your friends and posting a short review on Amazon. Word of mouth is an author's best friend.

Please Click Here to Leave a Review

Also, it would be my honor to have you join my mailing list. As my gift to you for joining, you will receive 3 **free** short stories and my USA Today award-winning novella complimentary in your email! To sign up, just go to my website at www.RobertaKagan.com

I send blessings to each and every one of you,

Roberta

Email: roberta@robertakagan.com

ACKNOWLEDGMENTS

I would also like to thank my editor, proofreader, and developmental editor for all their help with this project. I couldn't have done it without them.

Paula Grundy of Paula Proofreader

Terrance Grundy of Editerry

Carli Kagan, Developmental Editor

CONTACT ME

I love hearing from readers, so feel free to drop me an email telling me your thoughts about the book or series.
Email: roberta@robertakagan.com
Please sign up for my mailing list, and you will receive Free short stories including an USA Today award-winning novella as my gift to you!!!!! To sign up...

Check out my website
http://www.robertakagan.com.
Come and like my Facebook page!
https://www.facebook.com/roberta.kagan.9
Join my book club
https://www.facebook.com/groups/
1494285400798292/?ref=br_rs
Follow me on BookBub to receive automatic emails whenever I am offering a special price, a freebie, a giveaway, or a new release. Just click the link below, then click follow button to the right of my name. Thank you so much for your interest in my work.

https://www.bookbub.com/authors/roberta-kagan.

Made in the USA
Monee, IL
19 February 2023

28245610R00083